GISELLE

CARMEN ROSALES

ISBN 9798467968698

TRIGGER WARNING

This story contains content that might be troubling to some readers, including, but not limited to, rape, death, references of death, suicide, self-harm, vivid nightmares, bad language, abuse, child hood trauma, and PTSD. Please be mindful of these and other possible triggers. Seek help if needed and do not read. This is a dark romance and if these types of scenes or references trouble you **please do not read.**

1

GISELLE

"One, two, three, and up pirouette, back down." I remember the best way to start the movement is in the fourth position. My instructor at Juilliard is making sure we are all perfect as one unit, in synch in one of the hardest movements to conduct in sequence. We have been at it for the past hour. I can see the other girls' faces and they are tired, but I'm not. I love all things dance. My mom saw me watching a recital with admiration and awe in my eyes when I was five. She immediately enrolled me in a small dance academy in South Dakota and I have been dancing ever since. Jazz, dance, ballet, and contemporary dance—I learned it all. I watched all things ballet and studied it; it's all I have been interested in since I knew it existed.

My parents are hardworking; my mother a schoolteacher, and my father runs a farm. I was never into farming, just into horses. I learned how to ride, but that's about as far as my interest went back home living on the farm.

My parents were savers and did not splurge on the finer things in life. The only allowance they gave me was when I helped around the house or on the farm. I worked for everything, but they taught me values and never let me give up on my dream to be accepted into Juilliard. I danced every day until I auditioned, and then I got accepted—to one of the most prestigious dance schools in the world, no less.

New York is a far cry different from Houghton, South Dakota, but I learned to grow a thick skin. New York is a beautiful city with bright lights, glamour and fashion. Your dreams can come true, or it can leave you pinching pennies to make rent. I was promised a career in dance. I already had a spot on the dance company and possibly in theater. I have prepared and concentrated my whole life on dance and the ballet, to receive flowers after finishing a performance at the American Ballet Theatre. To be a professional ballerina. It's my dream, and I'm so close I can taste victory. This is my last year as a senior at Juilliard. They say I am one of the best they have seen in a while, but I am humble enough to know there are other girls, even guys, who are just as good. I have never been the snobbish type to think I am better than anyone. My parents taught me to believe in myself, and to never let success go to your head.

I listen to my instructor as she calls my name in front of the class.

"Giselle! I want you to finish the piece with a fouetté," she says. I nod, understanding what she wants. She wants to save the hardest move for last, a move I have perfected since I was fifteen.

"Yes, madame," I respond.

Our instructor for ballet is French, and she insists we call her madame. I thought it funny here in New York, but wanting a career in dance or in the company, I will embrace the French culture and comply. I studied all there is on the culture of dance and ballet, even hip hop, pop, rap, especially music. Lana Del Rey is my favorite artist to create dance moves and choreography for my contemporary pieces.

I was homeschooled for high school at my mom's instruction. My parents told me if I wanted a shot at Juilliard, then they would have to pay for extra lessens during the weekdays at the dance academy. I would have no time for school or a real social life. It is one sacrifice I had to make. I wanted, deep down, to have a social life in high school, to have friends, and maybe a serious boyfriend; all the things a teenage girl dreams of, but I chose my calling and passion. I had to put those wants and needs on the back burner. My mom would have a mom to daughter talk every so often, making sure homeschooling and Juilliard is what I really wanted, and if I changed my mind, all I had to do was say the word and they would both understand. There was really nothing they could say to change my mind. Even if I had a crazy doubt, all the money and sacrifices they made just for me, so I could fulfill my dream as a little girl, would have been for nothing. I used to hate being an only child, but I knew I was blessed to have the best parents in the world, and being a selfish daughter isn't who I am.

They blessed me in the looks department with chocolate brunette hair and green eyes. Since I didn't have siblings, I couldn't call a sister or brother. I had my best friend at the trailer park just down the road, Brielle. I would call her Brie for short. We hit it off in elementary school when I would sit with her at lunch. No one wanted to be her friend because of her mom. Her mom was the town whore, and everyone thought she would end up just like her. I felt terrible for her on most days as I watched her eat lunch on her own. Kids can be cruel sometimes and would make fun of her mom to her face or behind her back. It didn't stop in middle school, but only got worse in high school.

She would come home with tears streaming down her face and sobbing. I would comfort her and tell them they were assholes and were just immature. She would tell me that the guys would think she was a just like her mother just because one day she gave her virginity to Jace when he asked her out.

They were dating her whole sophomore year and once they had sex, he dumped her. I was there for her when she would just come over and cry. He made up stories of how she would let him and his friend have a threesome with her. A total asshole in my book.

He continued to spread rumors that her mom didn't care, and because her mom was a whore, that's why she didn't know who her father was. She said I was lucky to have parents like mine and that she wished her mom wasn't the way she was. If Brie's mom would just be a decent mom and get a good job, maybe they wouldn't have to live in the trailer.

"Giselle," my instructor drawls in her French accent. Surprised and lost in my head, not realizing I was up for the fouetté.

"Oh, I'm so sorry Madame." I walk up to the center of the stage in haste and execute the fouetté effortlessly. I know I nailed it, but if you looked at my instructor's face, you would think I flopped. You never know what that woman is thinking. She keeps such a straight face and stern demeanor, never cracking a smile.

When the class is over, I rush out to head to the girls' dorms to take a shower. My feet are killing me. That's one downside of being in dance and ballet—our toes take a beating, and I need to dip them in bath salts to prevent further damage. I hardly wear sandals because it is pointless to get a pedicure. One of the many things that are overlooked. Dancers have magnificent physiques, but lack in the feet department. I keep my toenails cut super short, and it has worked just fine.

2
NATE

I walk into the gym ready for my workout session and immediately see my best friend and manager, Jaden.

"There you are! I have been waiting," he says.

"I'm here, aren't I?"

"Dude, why you sound pissed?"

"Nothing. I'm just in a mood and need to let off steam." Jaden is my best friend and he doesn't know about my innermost feelings. I don't talk about the demons that come out to play at night in my head, reminding me where I came from, or how I got here. I have always had nightmares since I was kid, but they have become stronger the longer it takes for my next fight to come.

My next fight is a month away and I can't wait to feel the crack of bone and the smell of blood spilled in the cage. I feed off of it, calming the rage built up inside, needing to be unleashed. My nightmares are the same, different scenes playing out from my childhood. My dad beating my mother and my mother taking another hit off the needle to dull the pain. Heroin is a bitch to come back from, even when you go to rehab. Some people make it, and some don't. My mother didn't. She died of an apparent overdose, or it could have been from blunt force trauma from my dad beating her. So, when she was gone, he took his rage out on me.

One night I came home from school, walking down the sidewalk at eight years old, and noticed my dad's old beat-up truck in the driveway. I found it odd that he was home this early. He usually got home around midnight from drinking at the bar. Because as much as he smokes meth, he is also an alcoholic, coming home usually finding my mom passed out on the couch from her last hit. If he found her like that, he slapped her awake, and if she wakes, she is lucky to just endure slaps instead of punches. I reached the door to find it unlocked and the stench of death in the air from my father's last hit.

"Get up, you stupid bitch!" he snarls. "Where is the money you stole from me?"

I look in the living room to see my mother passed out, her body on the couch with one strap of her dirty tank top falling down one shoulder while her eyes look into space. My father is over her, slapping her repeatedly. He is spitting as he screams at her with his filthy jeans and dirty mechanic shirt. My parents were drug addicts. I wonder how I wasn't born with birth defects from all the drugs and alcohol my parents consumed.

When the front door creaks open, my father turns to find me watching them from door. "What the fuck are doing standing there, boy? Close the fucking door, you scrawny piece of shit." I close the door quickly to avoid him getting angrier.

"So-so-rry, sir," I stammer.

"Well, hurry and go to your room before I beat you silly."

"Yes, sir."

Running to my room, I leave the door slightly open so I can see if I needed to help my mom. I was always afraid that one night he would hit her so hard he'd kill her. I continue to look through the crack of the door and I watch my father punch and slap my mother repeatedly, trying to wake her up. He grabs her, and she falls lifeless to the floor. He stomps on her face. Tears beginning to pool in my eyes and slowly stream down my face. I look down, noticing that I just peed on my only good pair of pants. I knew I would get a beating from my father once he found out. I realize that my mother isn't moving, her face is indescribable from all the times he hit her. I open the door and run out to stop him and he pushes me off of him, hitting the wall with a thud. I get up, adrenaline coursing through my veins to get him to stop. I know something is terribly wrong. I scream, telling him to stop. He looks up with an evil look in eyes.

"So maybe it was you who took the money. She probably spent it on you, filthy mongrel, always eating and shitting. You are no good and you will be nothing but a scrawny piece of shit," he spits.

"Something is wrong with her! She's not moving!" I scream. He looks down as realization dawns. He looks up with his blood-shot eyes high on meth.

"Call 911 and tell them that someone broke in. If you don't lie, I will kill you. You know she was high on that shit, and probably took too much. You better do as I say, or you will pay. Do you understand me?"

"Ye-s, sir," I stammer in fear, breathing rapidly, trying to get to the only phone in the small house to dial 911 with shaking hands and fingers.

"911, what your emergency?" the operator asks. I speak into the big phone and say the only thing that I was told to.

"Please, my mom is not moving, I-I-I think someone broke in and hurt her," I say, as clear as the sobs wracking my body would allow. When the operator instructs that the police and ambulance are on their way, the phone falls from my fingers and I stare as my father acts like he's trying to save my mother until help arrives. I look at him with fear and loathing, realizing that the one responsible for my mother's death is my father, and I just helped him cover up the fact.

"Come on, Nate. Combo and then south paw," Jaden says, while warming up on the bag. I hit it harder and harder. I have been at it for the past four hours. The team at the gym is watching in awe, and I don't take a break. That's what happens when I play out my mother's death and how I covered it up in my mind in fear of my father. Over and over I hit the bag, imagining it being my father's body as my muscles strain and bunch up with the effort. Every time I'm in the cage, it's exhilarating, a cleansing of my past, that nothing—or no one—can quench. I continue the onslaught on the bag and I switch to roundhouse kicks. I don't stop until I can't feel my arms on my six-foot-two frame, exhausted. I'm drenched in sweat and can't wait to hit the shower in the locker room.

My cage name, The Reaper, as in the Grim Reaper, is meant for show, but all fighters that have challenged me for my title have basically ended their career trying to take it, unable to defeat me. Like the Grim Reaper, deep down inside, I am no different. I do what I have to do and run with my team. I am no saint; more like the devil from the things I have done. I have to defend my title to some Brazilian fighter named Santos that thinks he can defeat me.

Yeah, we'll see how long he can last in the cage from a take-down or a beating. There are times they have to remove me after they tap out and my fans roar as I scream like an animal.

After a win, I have sponsors, commercials, and let's not forget—the women. They throw themselves at me and I can't say I don't have fun, but then they get clingy, thinking they have a chance. They complain, calling me cold-hearted and shallow, I just send them off with a care package in the morning. The tabloids picked up on it and made a whole article about how the millionaire pro MMA fighter sends his one-night stands with a care package in the morning. The fans ate that shit up. Instead of scaring the girls off, it only increased their attention to me. I couldn't care less, but after this fight, I already have another lined up, but I need a break in between, and preferably somewhere where there is no media. The paparazzi have been getting more aggressive since my last four wins and the fact that I broke my cardinal rule of sleeping with a girl more than once. Her name was Sabrina and she told them we were a couple and that we were going steady. When I found out, I fucking lost it with her. She was at my last fight, hoping I would tell her to come home with me, and when the media asked for a brief interview, she was waiting, and I made sure to let the whole world know that she was just a clingy bitch that wouldn't leave me alone, and to get off my dick. She tried to slap me, and I grabbed her wrist in a tight grip, looking menacingly in her face. I suddenly smiled at the camera. "See, folks. I told you she is delusional and won't leave me alone."

I can hear myself from the big screen TV re-airing my last fight. I stand as I watch myself smile, showing my straight, white teeth.

"Well there you have it, folks. Nate 'The Reaper' is, in fact, single and available," I hear the reporter say.

Great, I mutter to myself. *Now they really won't leave me alone.* I can't wait 'til the fight so I can take a week off to some place Jaden has suggested in South Dakota.

Just him and I alone, none of the team are going. Jaden has been with me since I started fighting at the Y, learning all the martial arts there is to know. When I made it to foster care at age thirteen, I started street fighting for cash. My fights went viral and landed in the hands of a promoter, and that's how I made it to MMA. I had to train hard and clean my skill up. Most of my moves were illegal in MMA at the time, but I've learned. Now I'm here on top of the world as one of the most successful pro MMA fighters. I started my gym teaching young inner-city kids to defend themselves and keep them off the street. Some of them are from broken homes with drug-addicted parents, like mine. I want to make a difference, I knew what it felt like to not have a stable home, or the love of a parent.

My father died after he owed money to some drug dealers. They came to collect while I was at school in the sixth grade. Child services came and put me in foster care. I have no family and no siblings. The only person I have who resembles a brother is Jaden; he comes from a similar background. His parents were just drug addicts, they didn't beat him like my father beat me.

My mother didn't hit me though. She was too high on heroin to beat me.

I basically only ate because of the public school system. I was a scrawny kid until they placed me in foster care. They made fun of me in middle school until I started street fighting, then I got respect. No one messed with me, unless they wanted a beat-down at an old warehouse that set up fights from the drug dealers in town. Yeah, I knew everyone selling drugs. They never messed with me, though. They knew my mother supposedly overdosed and was beaten up by some drug dealers coming to collect. No one knew the whole truth about how my mother died, and to be honest, no one gave a shit about a heroin addict. My father continued to beat me after my mother died. It got worse as I got older. There was a time when I thought I could take him, I think I was eleven and was getting taller, but when someone is on meth, it's like they have this super strength, and they don't stop until you're either unconscious, or dead. That didn't end well until he knocked me out. He would torture me by waking me up, burning cigarette butts on my inner thighs so no one at school could see the angry burn marks. I tried to wake up earlier, but he would beat me to it.

Sometimes at night, I wake up thinking a cigarette burned me. I tell no one that shit and that's why I don't let women sleep over. I sometimes wake up ready to swing and punch whoever, but there is no one there, just the dead silence of my empty home decorated by an interior designer.

For show, it's all for show. If anyone really knew how I lived when I was a kid, with no sheets on a mattress that was just thrown on the floor in a roach-infested room, they would probably feel sorry for me and then think I was lucky.

My house now is a palace compared to where I really grew up, with a shitty childhood filled with hate and violence. It's all I know, I was never loved by a mother or taught by a father. I was the mistake my mother told me I was. Telling me that, because of me, is why my father was so angry at her. She never hit me though, and told me to stay quiet and out of the way. I at least respected her for that. She was fucked up, just like I am, but in a different way. She chose drugs, and I choose fighting.

I walk outside the gym, waving at Charles.

"Have a great evening, champ!" he says.

"Thanks, Charles. Don't forget to lock up."

"No problem, boss. I'll lock up." I walk up to my bike; I like taking my bike on most days to avoid attention in my Lamborghini. Everyone looks at it with the modifications I made to it, adding body kits and mods. I wanted it to be unique, something no one else had. I used to dream of having a car like that when I was a kid. When I made my first million, it was one of the first things I bought.

I straddle my bike and grab my helmet with the tinted visor. I turn the matte-black super bike on, revving the engine, the smell of gas rising from the modified exhaust. God, I love the smell of my bike. It gives me the adrenaline rush I need to feel, to let off steam. I like to get home exhausted, so the darkness can take me to a blissful sleep. When I'm that tired, the nightmares don't usually come. I rev the engine again, going faster, speeding through the lanes with my headphones on, listening to *Sweet Dreams* by Marylin Manson on my way home.

3
GISELLE

The next day I make it to all my classes and I'm nervous about my contemporary piece I have been working on. I talk to the girls I have choreographed the piece with, and they are just as excited as I am. We help each other and I thank my lucky stars my parents always taught me to get along. I never had a social life except for Brie and some friends she would have over when my parents said it was okay. I miss her so much, but we still keep in touch at least once a week. The last time we spoke was last week, and she said she was living in Sioux Falls, and we should catch up soon. Her mom, Victoria, is still living in the trailer back home up to no good. I'm happy she made it out on her own with no support from her mom. She is a strong girl, and I will always be her friend if she needs me.

"Are you ready, Giselle?" one girl asks. Her name is Suzy. She is one of the better dancers that can keep up with my routines.

"Yeah. I mean, we have gone over it so many times in the past month, I just hope it's good enough," I tell her.

It's a contemporary piece and I hope it wows my instructors. I have taken a lot of time to choreograph the routine and decided to choose the orchestral version of *Young and Beautiful* by

Lana Del Rey. We take center stage after giving them my song to play. The four of us take our place. I am at the center, looking at the five judges, while Dean, a friend I have made here at Julliard, is behind the tripod with his camera. He wants to be a film editor and conductor. I have agreed to let him record my pieces. It will allow me to see where I need to make some adjustments and perfect my movements.

"Are you ready, miss Monroe?" the male judge asks impatiently.

"Yes, sir," I say.

"Well, let's get started. Since you have taken part in the ballet company, all they will require you to complete is the contemporary dance piece choreographed by yourself to show us in your final year how you have improved from a pre-professional standpoint. It will show us that you possess the required skill and talent you lead us to believe. It is your senior piece," he says.

"Yes, I am aware," I say, my voice echoing in the theater room with tiny beads of sweat running down my back, knowing what is on the line. It's what we all have worked for, all of us in my senior class. We know helping each other succeed is looked upon for selection to the best dance companies. *No sweat,* I tell myself. I look at the girls waiting for my cue and for the music to begin. I give the signal with my fingers, and at once, the chorus of Lana fills the speakers of the giant theater room. Her soft ballad hitting my soul, we all move in synch on our toes, two of us one way, the other girls moving their legs in a split in the air, before coming on our toes to the center, back in the start position. I have chosen the four of us who can complete a fouetté on cue at the fourth position, and bam! We nail it. I keep my face concentrated while moving on to the next move as we tourner (to turn) and they give me space to complete my move on my own, known as the grande jete. It is the most difficult jump, and if you don't stretch properly, you can get seriously injured. Flexibility is the key to the move. The girls give me space, and I execute the jump and nail it. I am so excited, it was the ultimate move, and we get in the same position as we started. We all stop in unison, and bow for the judges.

Dean suddenly screams, "Yes! Woo-hoo, that's my girl." I smile at his excitement. He pauses, and he realizes that his camera is still on. He clears his throat. "I am so sorry," he says, packing his stuff up to get the heck out of the theater.

I watch him scurry as he will most likely get kicked out by the judges. I hope the performance was good enough. I pause, waiting for further instruction.

"Miss Monroe?" the judge, who I'm assuming is in charge of the end of the senior piece performances, says.

"Yes," I respond. Aware I'm holding my breath, I let it out slowly, nervous as hell.

"That was exquisite, and we expected it from you. Perfection. I can safely say that, off the record, that was one of the best performances I have ever seen from a senior. You can very well run your own dance company someday, young lady." Relieved, my heartbeat slows down.

"That is very kind of you to say, sir. Thank you, that means a lot." He doesn't say a word, his serious face in place. I take my cue and leave with the other girls from the stage. I get out into the hallway, thanking them and hugging them tight.

"Thank you! You guys are the best, and if I can help anyone of you, please ask." They all smile at me, telling me that they already have their group picked out.

"You are the best ballet dancer here at Julliard, Giselle. Really. No bullshit. There is no way any of us could have nailed it, not even our instructor," Suzy says, whispering.

My face flushes. "No way,"

"Yes way. Seriously, you are so talented, you should see your face when you dance. It has passion written all over it. It's like you are one with the music," she says. My eyes fill with tears, feeling overjoyed at her compliment. I hug her suddenly.

"Shit. I'm so sorry," I say. I got carried away and she stands there in shock.

"No worries, I wasn't ready for a hug, is all." I smile, embarrassed because I don't really know her on a friendly level.

I thank them all and continue to the dorms. As I walk down the hallway, I spot Dean. He has sandy blonde hair, dimples on his cheeks, and blue eyes. He is handsome in a boyish sort of way. We have become fast friends this year when he came up to me to ask if he could film me dancing. He said he wanted to be a film editor and requested to film some of the girls for our senior year. In return, we would get an edited recording of our dances that could help us out in the future. How could anyone refuse a free copy of their pieces?

"You were exceptional!" he says.

I smile. "Thank you, Dean, that is so nice of you to say." He looks at me and I think he might have a crush on me, but I think he's just being Dean.

"I'm sorry I shouted in the theater in front of the judges when you were done. I don't know what came over me. I hope it didn't affect your grade." I notice he has a worried look in his eye.

"Oh, don't be silly. It was nothing. I am glad someone was cheering for me."

His eyes light up, relieved he didn't mess up my grade. He smiles at me, showing his cute dimples. "Hey, are you doing anything later?" he asks. I swallow. I knew it was coming, eventually asking me out. I feel bad about letting him down. I just don't have time to date anyone or anything like that. It's what has kept me focused here at Julliard. Sure, I had kissed before when Brie has brought over some high school friends to ride horses on my parent's farm.

One afternoon, in the summer of what should have been my

sophomore year, Brie brought Jason over. He was a junior at Harlow High. I was supposed to attend Harlow High, but since I was homeschooled due to dance, I knew none of the high school kids Brie hung out with. My parents allowed them over in the summers and long weekends so I could socialize with kids my age.

I am riding my favorite horse, Jasmine, and Jason is riding Onyx. We had decided to go horseback riding. We tether the horses to a tree so we can give them a break, and we start talking about what we were planning to do after high school. He suddenly gets close when no one else is nearby. He looks around, making sure we are far away from the barn so no one can see us. Brie and the others are riding by the stream on the other side. Jason suddenly draws closer, moving a strand of hair behind my ear. He is a foot taller than me, with green eyes and brown hair a shade lighter than my own. I notice up close that he had a light dusting of freckles on his nose.

"Giselle?" he says.

"Yes," I say softly, looking up into his green eyes. What I find there is desire. I know at this moment that he wants to kiss me. I find him nice and attractive, but I don't feel the pull I had read about in books or watched in movies. He's just Jason, a friend who would come over to hang out with Brie and her other friends.

"I am going to kiss you," he says. His head angles toward me and his lips hover just above mine.

"Okay," I whisper.

Not protesting or denying him, I want to feel what it would be like to get kissed by a boy. I know if I don't let him, I would probably never experience what it's like. He isn't mean. He treats me nicely, so I don't think much of it. His lips continue to hover over mine slowly, and I close my eyes. When I feel the softness of his lips, my hands automatically go around his neck, as I have seen so many girls do when they're kissed. He pulls me close while his tongue teases my lips, holding me by the waist, I allow him to slide his tongue inside, tasting me. I stand there, not knowing what I'm doing, and let him take the lead. He continues to kiss my mouth, and when I can't breathe any more, he breaks the kiss, letting me get air.

I smile, releasing my hands from his neck breathlessly. I place my fingers on my now swollen lips and smile at him. He stands, looks at me, and steps away, like the kiss never happened. I feel deflated. Maybe I'm not a good kisser, and he didn't like it. I stop smiling at him and frown as he moves to give me the reins of my horse. I look at him, confused at his sudden behavior; he could have been a little nicer about it.

"Is there something wrong?" I ask him.

"No, nothing. We should head back." He moves to help me on the horse, and I move out of his grasp.

"I don't need your help, I'm fine," I snap. I turn away, not looking at him.

"Look, I was just helping you out," he says.

"Well, I don't need your help, and for the record, don't ever fucking kiss or touch me again," I snap.

Taking off with Jasmine back to the barn, leaving him alone with Onyx by the tree, I don't look back. I didn't feel any spark or anything from the kiss. It was just a kiss, but my pride got the best of me when he suddenly turned cold like it was the worst possible kiss he had ever experienced. I place Jasmine in the barn and run into the house. Closing the door to my bathroom, I slide down the door with tears streaming down my face. That was the first and only kiss I had ever experienced, and I knew in that moment I wouldn't miss high school.

The following weekend, Brie and I go to a local hangout all the high school kids go to after a football game. Football is a big deal where I come from. Businesses would close early just to make it to the game. It gave the town something to do with the full spirit of tradition.

We make it to the taco spot, and all the football players and popular kids are there. Brie and I are walking to make the line, laughing at a joke we heard from a movie we had watched the other day, when we pass a table with Jace, and Jason. Jason looks up, and he stops talking to Jace when he notices me walking with Brie. His eyes are on me, not trying to hide the fact that I can see him looking directly at me. Jace stops in mid-

sentence to see what has caught Jason's attention. He looks at Brie and me.

"Oh, it's the hoe and the virgin. How ironic." Brie and I stop when everyone turns to see who Jace is referring to. They all look at us, listening to what Jace, the star quarterback of the football team, is saying. My eyes widen in shock as I stand, not believing that he just called Brie a hoe and me a virgin. I look at Jason. He is also on the football team, as a tight end. His expression reveals nothing as he just looks at me. They both have full ride scholarships to a D1 school, hopefully making it to the NFL.

"Hey Jason, how was it kissing the virgin? It must have been nice to win the bet. Who could kiss the virgin little dancer? Nice way to make fifty bucks. I would have agreed now looking at her, she's a fine piece of ass. Shit, I should have taken the bet."

What an asshole. I don't know what Brie saw in him. I want to climb over the table and claw both their eyes out, the bastards. My intention is short-lived because everyone laughs at us. I look at Brie and her eyes are brimming with unshed tears, and I give Jace and Jason a murderous glare.

"Fuck you! Both of you, pieces of shit!" I yell at them with rage. Everyone stops laughing, wondering what they will say next, but to everyone's surprise, they stay stunned at my reaction. The good girl has a mouth, to their utter shock.

I grab Brie's hand, "Let's go, Brie. Don't get upset, it was wrong coming here and ruining our girl's night out watching the evidence of a regretful mistake you just want to forget. They're not worth it," I say out loud. I see both Jace and Jason's face turn serious, not expecting me to throw it back in their faces. Shocked with some of their mouths hanging open, we leave, and I vow to never allow them over my house again.

"So, how about it? Go out with me later?"

I shake my head. "What?" I ask, looking at Dean. I totally forgot what he asked me. He brought back memories from the past; vivid and surreal. I swore to myself that I wouldn't date or trust anyone with my feelings. Look what happen last time. "I-I don't think that's a great idea, Dean."

I hated letting him down. He seems so nice, but I remember

one guy that kissed me who acted the same way. Dean's face looks so sad, but he shakes it off in understanding. "I get it. I know you have a goal here. No distractions, right?" I smile as he understands.

"Exactly!" I just want to be friends and I hope he understands, and doesn't go acting all weird on me because I turned him down.

"Okay, can we still hang out as friends around campus?" he asks.

"Of course," I say. I walk toward my dorm room as I feel my phone vibrate with an incoming call from a weird number I don't recognize. I answer the phone. "Hello?"

"Yes. Is this miss Monroe, daughter of Mr. and Mrs. Monroe?"

"Yes."

"Hello, I know you are in New York, but you must come back home. My name is Officer Chandler. I hate to say this to you, miss Monroe, but there has been a car accident on the interstate and your parents didn't make it."

All I hear is a strong ringing in my ears as I drop my phone and fall to my knees. I don't see or hear anything except a loud scream that I think is coming from my mouth. Everything goes black and I all I feel are powerful arms trying to hold me up. I think it's Dean trying not to let me fall and hurt myself. I stay there on my knees, not knowing for how long, and all I can hear is ringing and the deep thump of my heartbeat. I hear footsteps as the staff guide me up and assist me back to my dorm room. Dean has my phone, and he is speaking into it. I still can't get the ringing and thumping from my ears to go away as I am laid down on my dorm room bed.

4

GISELLE

I make it back home and I have to sell everything; the farm, the house, animals...everything. I am left with five thousand dollars to my name, just enough to find a place and get a job. I can't go back to New York. When I finished settling my parent's debts, they had already replaced my spot on the dance company. I, at least, graduated from Julliard because—thank God—my performance was good enough. There was no dream job waiting for me back there. My dream died the same day my parents did. It has left me with nothing, and no family; I don't have a brother or sister. The only friends that came through were Brie and Dean to make sure I held up. Brie came to pick me up, so I could move in with her temporarily, until I could find a decent apartment. She even pulled some strings at a local diner so I could have a job to support myself. I couldn't thank her enough. I haven't practiced dance for almost two months, and honestly, mourning both my mother and father's death is hard enough. Hearing the blaring of a horn, I look into my childhood home for the very last time as tears threaten to fall down my cheeks. I breathe in deep, and close the door with a thud.

I grab my only suitcase with all my possessions and walk toward Brie's car with the windows down.

"You need help with that?" she asks.

"I got it, but thanks for asking." I place it in the back seat of her old, beat-up Ford. I open the passenger door and slide in. I turn to her and give her a tight hug, holding back the tears once more before I cry for the millionth time.

"It's okay, Giselle," she says, rubbing my back. I hug her just as fiercely, needing someone's support and love. I close my eyes shut, hoping this is just a bad dream and when I open them, everything will be back to normal. When I open my eyes, of course, the nightmare is still here, and my parents are no longer with me. I can't call my mom or dad and tell them how my day went, or if I met a guy. I'm so heartbroken and alone, all my dreams lost, feeling empty inside with just despair, and utter loneliness.

"Alright, let's get to Sioux Falls," she says. Brie has been living there for the past three years now, only twenty miles from my parents' home. She works at the diner during the day, and at night she describes how she dances at a strip club/dance club that a hot shot developer from Las Vegas built. State-of-the-art lighting and sound system, the stage has three dance poles and a handful of dancers, some strip and others wear skimpy outfits, but don't really take their close off. "Hey, I was thinking. You should be our choreographer and teach us some new routines to bring in new clients. The clients lately are all rich and mostly sport celebrities. We need one more girl who doesn't strip. It's a spot that hasn't hit the mainstream media yet, and the people that hang out there spend enough money to not want the publicity."

"I don't know, Brie. I will not take my clothes off or do other stuff for money."

"Then don't," she quips.

"Aww Brie, I didn't mean it like that. I know you don't go all nude and there are some regulars that you actually don't mind doing extra dances for, but I just never thought about creating routines for that type of dance." She smiles, laughing.

"I was just kidding, Giselle. Of course, I'm not mad. I just figured you needed to get your mind off stuff and needed a release. The girls would love you, and with your skills, it would be a win-win for all of us there. We would pack the house and you'd only have to dance three times a week."

"Okay. Why not? Talk with the owner and let me know what he and the manager say."

"I kind of already did," she says.

I look at her, wide eyed. "Holy shit. I already got the job?"

"Well, of course. You're a bad bitch at dancing, Giselle, and if I vouch for you, then it must be true."

"Okay, fine. On one condition: You guys teach me how to pole dance," I say excitedly.

She turns to glance at me. "Deal."

We get to her apartment and it's small; really only for one person. I find the leasing manager and I am just in luck. There is an apartment available. The couple living there needs a bigger place because they're having a kid. She tells me it will be available in three days because the place needs to be to cleaned and painted. I'm so excited to have my own place in the same building as Brie. I really need the job at the club she mentioned called *The Porcelain Dollhouse*. An interesting name. Brie says all the girls that are selected to work there are beautiful, like porcelain dolls.

I can't wait to learn how to pole dance. I love everything that has to do with dancing, even though my parents would turn in their graves if they found out. Feels crazy thinking that they're not around to call me anymore or wonder if I'm okay. I think the club will be good for me right now. I head over to Brie's apartment after leaving the leasing manager's office and knock on her door. She opens immediately, smiling and hugging me.

"Oh my gosh, Giselle. This is going to be so much fun living and working in the same place." I smile in her embrace, smelling her fruity body splash from her long blonde hair and look into the pretty blue eyes of my best friend in the universe.

"I'm excited, too. And couldn't do this without your help. I'm so grateful to have two jobs to pay for all my bills, and the best part is, I get to dance without being completely naked." I giggle.

"OMG, I know. Look, there is a back room that shit goes down in for VIP clients only, but you don't have to do that, or strip nude. They hire strictly to dance and perform special entertainment. If you ever go to the back room, you might learn some things." She laughs, giving me a wink.

I immediately blush, thinking about looking at girls having sex with guys who are willing to pay for it. I have never been into voyeurism, but out of curiosity, I wouldn't be offended at seeing people have sex in its raw form with no emotions attached. My understanding of sex is to fall for a guy and being in love, but never just for unemotional reasons or to feel good.

"I can't wait to try the pole dancing. First, I want to figure out how to climb up, slide down real fast, and stop just before hitting the ground. I saw it on the internet once when pole dancing was trending," I say.

“Okay. If you show me some bad ass dance routines with the right music, we can have this place jam packed on weekends with all the girls making money. They all have goals to save enough for college, business, buy a house, and never have to pay rent again. We all have goals, and this is just a stepping stone in achieving them from the guys that are willing to pay for entertainment.”

“I’m going to learn something I never thought I would learn. They don’t teach pole dancing at Juilliard, that’s for sure,” I say, laughing.

“Okay. I got your pretty pink uniform and name tag for the diner on Monday, and we have the weekend to teach you how to pole dance and perfect that move you mentioned, and start us on some dance routines.”

The next day, we arrive at the club, and I meet the manager, the girls, and Chris, the head security guy at the door. He’s the guy you go to when there are customers who can’t keep their hands to themselves or cannot comprehend the word *no*. He runs a tight ship with ten other security bouncers just as big. The manager comes up; a lady in her fifties with business experience involving all things strip and dance clubs. I fill out all the paperwork and I am relieved my title says choreographer slash dancer.

“Okay miss Monroe, your stage name is going to have

Monroe in it, just need to find something catchy to go with it after your first night here. I will let you know what stage name that is, and you will be known to use that name. It is for your safety that you don't give the customers your real name, as some of them can get a little clingy in their made-up fantasies." I try not to giggle, but I know she's right, and saying it from experience, having been a dancer and stripper herself.

I come up with a few dance routines for the evening, then try and teach it to the girls, and they all catch on quickly. They teach me how to pole dance with the basic moves and I nail them perfectly. I even learn how to slide down the pole effortlessly, thanks to the years of dance training. The girls, Diamond, Treasure, and even Brie, say I'm a pro at it. It excited them for the last 7 hours with all the dances we practiced. When its 10:00 p.m., the club opens its doors. I also meet the DJ, Jake, he spins at the club every night. He explains that the girls get to choose the music for their dance routine unless there is a special request from a customer for a particular girl. It gets the customers engaged, and that means they spend more money. I practice my dance routine and when I'm finished, Jake watches me.

"Your very talented," he says.

"Thank you, Jake, that is very nice to say. I am sure you are talented as well if you're the only one hired here to spin."

Just like Brie described, the club has one of the best neon lighting systems that changes in synch with the music, including lasers, black lights, and three tall dance poles that reach high into the warehouse-type building. The height makes the stage appear bigger than what it really is, but has the added advantage of space in front so the girls can complete dance moves, and strip without hitting themselves with the metal poles.

He smiles at me. "So, I know you're from here, but where did you go to school?" he asks.

"Upstate, I graduated and was offered a job, but my parents

passed, and I had to move back and settle their debts on top of burying them. It was the hardest thing I have had to do. So, here I am."

"I'm sorry about your parents," he says. I look down, my face showing the hurt it still gives me when I think about them. He changes the subject quickly. "So, who is your absolute favorite artist?" he asks.

My eyes light up. "Well, Lana Del Rey, of course." I say. He looks up from setting up his equipment with his black hair, and brown eyes.

"I can see that is definitely your style, with a lot of seductive sex appeal. Now I know what to play when you're up there on your own," he says.

"Thank you, I trust your judgment. The DJ is just as good as the dancers," I say.

I get ready with the girls in the dressing room. I went with Brie into town and bought a couple of bras and matching lace panties to go with the sexy costumes. They have so many beautiful ones, it was hard to choose. I have two dance routines for the night on short notice, each of us will take turns on our solos, except for Brie and I, we don't go all nude in the club. When we're not dancing, we're serving, and according to Brie, the money is substantial. We have to go by our stage name at the club, so I have to call Brie, Coco.

The club fills up quickly with some couples, but mostly men, while Jake spins the latest hip-hop and dance. I notice a few celebrity ball players, football players, and even hockey players, all in the section where mostly the VIP are seated. I notice a hooded figure, along with a guy wearing a white T-shirt, jeans, and a hat with all of his tattoos on display. They take a seat in the middle while I can hear people calling out, "*Good fight, champ.*" Must be a fighter or something, but I can't really see his face. I'm not into boxing or MMA. It's not a big deal in my hometown, unlike football. Football is the soul of my hometown.

The fighter and his friend sit at the section Brie and I are in charge of for the night. I get a tray and walk up to them, dressed in garters and a very short skirt with my butt on display along with a tight corset that pushes my breasts up, making my very generous rack look even bigger. I have the typical stripper shoes on that are not uncomfortable, but make your legs look long and appealing. My hair is in waves down my back, wearing light makeup, not overdoing it, for fear of the sweat that will drip down my face from dancing. I come up to their table with Coco by my side to help me out and get their orders. Seeing both men slouching in their chairs, I almost trip over their long legs. The hooded figure looks up and removes his hoodie, revealing light brown hair, a two-day-old bearded shadow, and the most intense hazel eyes I have ever seen. I look at his friend with his faded haircut, but I don't look into his eyes because my focus is on the guy they call 'champ.' I see his knuckles are rough with scabs on them, his face without a scratch, and his small, straight nose. He is breathtakingly beautiful and should model instead of fight.

"Welcome to The Porcelain Dollhouse, what can we get you boys?" I ask. The fighter looks at me and then averts his eyes, dismissing me.

His friend smiles while looking at Coco and says, "Two beers, please." I write it down, feeling the fighter's eyes on my legs, looking at my thighs up to my skirt. Instantly, I feel aware of him and feel hot. I can't wait for my routine to take the corset off and be in just the bra and skirt with pantyhose hooked up to my garters.

"Okay, we will be back with your beers, and if you want anything else, just press this button on the table," I say, as I show him the wristwatch Coco and I wear, that alerts us whenever we are needed at our tables. The fighter doesn't say a word, and I decide I don't have time to be treated like crap on my first night, after everything that has happened.

"What are your names in case the button doesn't work?" the friendlier one asks.

"My name is Monroe, and my friend next to me is Coco." He winks at Coco and she smiles back at him, giving him a little wave. I turn with Coco to get their beers and then head back to Diamond.

Diamond is from Atlanta with her creamy brown skin and a huge butt that she loves to twerk. Coco and I will climb up the pole with the other girls flanking the side, with me in the middle. Diamond coming down first, twerking for the football players, and then I'll be up for my solo I have been working on for the past four hours. I give Jake Diamond's two selections to mix for the routine, *WAP* and *Don't Stop* by Megan Thee Stallion and Cardi B. Both songs are aggressive and not my choice, but in this place, it's appropriate.

Brie looks at me. "What?" I say.

"That is Nate 'The Reaper' and his manager," Brie says with excitement.

"So?" I shrug my shoulders. "He was a total dick to us."

Diamond chimes in, "He is like that because women throw their panties at him all the time and I can see why. Girl, he is fine. And that body..." She gestures with her hands.

"Whatever." I wave my hand like it doesn't matter. I know he's very good-looking, but too intense, and was totally rude to me and Coco. I didn't throw myself at him, I was just doing my job, no matter how attractive I find him.

"He is undefeated, and he beat his last opponent in under a minute in the cage. The guy is a fucking badass in MMA," Diamond says.

I look at them both with determination. "Guess what? We are badass dancers going to make it rain in this fucking place," I say. We walk up to the stage and take our positions in front of the poles. We look at Jake with everyone's eyes on us, including Nate and his manager, as they sit up straighter in their chair, not believing their server is about to go on a stripper pole, after serving them their beers.

Jake signals the beginning of Diamond's routine as WAP plays through the amazing sound system in the club, the bass vibrating the whole place as the lyrics spill. We shake our ass out holding the pole, our backside facing the audience. I can hear catcalls as Diamond takes off her clothes. I bend over, touch my toes, shaking my butt, twerking, as does Coco. She and I climb the tall poles as *Don't Stop* plays, watching all the guys look up in awe, not believing what they are seeing, as Diamond follows suit. We reach the top, and at the right moment, everyone cheers as we hold the pole with our legs upside down, while our hair hangs. When the lyrics come at the hook, we loosen our thighs and slide in unison down the pole and skid to a halt just before we hit the ground, to a roaring crowd throwing tons of money in the air on stage. The three of us let go of the pole at the same time, standing to our feet and catwalk up the stage, popping and twerking to the song, until it comes to the end, ending up in the same position we started.

We hear whistling from the guys as they continue to throw money. "Well, well, I want to introduce you all to our best kept secret here at The Porcelain Dollhouse... Miss Money Monroe!" Jake says over the mic. The guys holler and continue to whistle as I get in place for my routine. I trust Jake to pick my song, as I didn't give him one.

I hear the sexy voice of Lana del Rey, singing *Fucked My Way to the Top*, as I go up on the pole and twirl, then up to the ceiling and down to the bottom, crawling on the stage. I remove my corset and I can see the fighter's eyes not leaving me for one second, as he follows my movements intently. His manager is watching him, looking back and forth as I continue to twirl in my bra, skirt, and garters on the pole, completing an upside-down split. The song changes into another song by Lana called *American*, a more of a ballet tune with her sexy voice. I go slow, twirling on the pole holding my hands in the center, splitting my legs into a full split in the air, facing the crowd while the men have their mouths open and Brie stands in awe...

She smiles, her eyes twinkling even from where I can see her about seven feet in the air, as I wrap my limbs around the pole and spread my hands, holding myself with just my thighs and calves. The bra straps slide down my shoulders as the song ends. Sliding down to my feet, grabbing my corset, as the song ends.

"Everyone, please give a round of applause for the beautiful and talented Miss Money Monroe. She made it rain!" Jake announces with pride. The hoots and catcalls vibrate over the music in the club.

"She doesn't even have to take off her clothes!" one guy shouts as I flush in embarrassment.

I feel the vibration of the watch from my table numbered 43, where the fighter is seated, as I put on a thin tank for a little decency. I have to get used being only in a bra while waiting tables. I thought I could just walk around in a bra, but suddenly feeling shy, I changed my mind.

Brie walks up to me and gives me a hug. "That was beautiful, Giselle," she whispers close to my ear.

I release her and smile. "Oh please, you guys were awesome. I was just doing the moves I learned recently."

"No way, sweetheart. It was like you mixed ballet with pole dancing and were one with the music. It was beautiful. Even Nate "The Reaper" was in awe. He couldn't stop looking at you. No different from any other male in the room," she says.

I kiss her cheek. "Well, we are being requested at the Reaper's table," I say as I show her my watch. Her eyes light up and we make our way to the table from the back.

We reach the table and I point upstairs to Jake on the DJ

booth, and I mouth a thank you and blow him a kiss he catches in the air and places on his chest. I catch the fighter's gaze as he looks at me and then at the DJ. He smirks at me as I look at his gorgeous face.

"How does your boyfriend feel about all the attention you get in this place?" he asks.

"I-I don't have a boyfriend," I stammer, but catch myself as I respond to him.

He raises his eyebrows, surprised. "How come?" he asks softly.

"How come what?"

"How come you don't have a boyfriend?"

I look directly in his eyes, honesty in my words. "Because I'm not interested in anyone?" I answer.

"Hmm," is all he mutters.

"Can I get you anything?" I show him my watch that I silenced.

"Yeah, you on his lap," his friend says, jokingly.

Surprised, I blush, my face turning red.

Coco is standing behind me as she interrupts him. "I'm sorry, but she doesn't do lap dances or any special services. She just dances," she says.

Nate, as he is called, looks at me after hearing her words. "So you don't lap dance, strip nude or do any special services, just dance?" he asks me directly.

"That's right, just dance. You seem disappointed," I say. I look at his friend for a clue but he sits back, listening to the conversation.

"Nah, I just realized you are just one big fat tease in this place." I suck in a breath, definitely taken aback by his coldness and insult. What did I expect? He is just like every guy who thinks too highly of himself. His type is the reason I don't date, or bother trying. For what? To be made fun of, judged, and treated like crap? I can hear Brie behind me wanting to tell him off, but I beat her to it, making sure I try to stay as professional as possible, so I don't lose my job on my first night.

I speak jokingly, but telling him the truth at the same time, "You know, I liked you better with your mouth shut and your hoodie on. It's a better look for someone like you," I tell him. His head snaps up, not expecting my snarky reply. I smile and cease all conversation with him, completely ignoring him and speaking directly with his manager about what they would like next, waiting for the night to be over.

* * *

The following night is Sunday. In the morning, Brie and I have the morning shift at the diner. Brie is getting ready for our night at the club. I just have one dance lined up, feeling a little sore from the previous night. Who knew pole dancing was quite the workout? Walking out the locker room, the doors open and the club is almost at full capacity, as more people come in through the door. I see Nate is back with his manager at the same table.

Great, I hope he just stays quiet. I will let Coco handle their orders tonight. I want to avoid him as much as possible. I can see him looking at me from the corner of my eye. I'm getting ready for my turn on stage, putting the dirty cups on the bar, when two familiar faces I haven't seen in a long while are next to me at one of Diamond's VIP tables. Trying to avoid them noticing me, I walk in between the tables, looking straight ahead. A hand grabs my wrist, halting me, and when I turn, I take in a deep breath. I look down to see Jason looking at me with his green eyes and a warming smile.

"I knew it was you," he says out loud. I turn to find Jace and my eyes turn cold. I look back at Jason, memories of our last encounter filtering in my mind.

"What do you want? Let go of me," I quip. Surprised at my reaction, he releases my hand.

"I'm sorry. I was just excited to see you here."

"Sure you are," I snap.

"Is she here, too?" Jace asks.

"That's none of your business. And do both yourselves a favor. Stay away from us."

"Oh, come on. It was a mistake what we said to you and Brie. We don't regret the other stuff though, that was real," Jason says tenderly.

"Well, news update. It was a mistake for me, so fuck off." I turn around, catching the eyes of both Nate and his manager, clearly engrossed in my little spat with Jace and Jason. I heard they play for the Ravens. They made it as pro football players, Jace the quarterback and Jason their starting tight end. Football in a small town is a big thing, and when one of their own makes it to the pros, it becomes well known.

Turning on my heels, I dismiss them and rush to the back as it's my cue to dance. I tell Brie about my brief encounter and her eyes go wide.

"You're shitting me," she says. I nod. I tell her about our little spat and the fact that we had an audience. I arrange my lace bodysuit under my robe with a matching short skirt and red fishnet thigh high stockings complete with calf-length boots that have a five-inch platform heel.

I hear Jack announce me. I gave him my two song choices of Lana Del Rey's, *Cola* and *This is What Makes Us Girls,* mixing it up, *Cola* being last. Echoing through the speakers, Jake's voice permeates through the entire club. "Get ready for the sexy and beautiful, Miss Money Monroe!"

I walk up in my robe, covering my body from what I am wearing underneath. My makeup is all sparkly under the lights, followed by Brie with mascara running down on her cheeks for show, acting like she's crying for *This What makes Us Girls,* the lyrics describing how boys make us cry and what makes us girls. I smile and blow a kiss to Jake and wave. The crowd cheers with catcalls on Coco and me, with her kneeling in front of the audience as I dance and twirl with different ballet moves without the need of slippers. I spin around her, dropping my robe, revealing my lace bodysuit and fishnets under the tiniest skirt. I point at Jace and Jason, making everyone notice they made her cry from the song. People boo at them and cheer when I remove her corset top, raising her to her feet so we can dance together as if we are a couple, we hold hands as we climb the same pole together, so we can slide down, her going first. I follow, skidding to a halt before hitting the glossy surface. No one at the club has attempted two girls on the same pole. We nail it perfectly as the crowd gives a round of applause.

Brie rushes from the stage and *Cola* begins as soon as I'm alone. I bend over, shaking my ass, removing a garter band from my thigh. I throw it at Nate. He catches it, and everyone wants one too, and I shake my finger in a seductive *no*. I look at Nate, as Jason looks over with jealousy. Nate smirks in his direction, twirling the band on his finger, showing off his prize. When the dance is over, the crowd cheers, throwing money in the air, falling like snow on a snow day. I walk down and place my robe over my half naked body, walking to my tables, asking if they require anything. Once I get to Nate and his manager, Nate looks at me and smiles with the whitest straight teeth I have ever seen. I think my panties are soaked as I instinctively squeeze my thighs together.

"I enjoyed that," he says.

"Really?" I ask, smirking at him.

"Absolutely, I loved that you gave me something everyone else wanted, especially when you told them no. Like that asshole over there." He points in Jason's direction. "He's lucky I didn't go over there and punch his fucking face in for looking at me when you threw this at me." He holds the garter band in the air as Jason looks over.

"Would you like to put it back on?" I tease. He smiles as he looks up my legs from my short robe as I slip it off.

"I would love to." He turns to the side, away from the table and I stand between his legs. He's wearing a black V-neck shirt, and I can see a bit of lettering from his chest tattoos along the deep cuts of his chest muscles. Up close, his face is even more beautiful than I initially thought.

"I'm going to hold on to your shoulder so I can lift my leg and you can slip it on. Is that okay?" I ask. He looks up at me and brings me close as he looks down, waiting for me to lift my leg, raising my high-heeled boot. I can't see his expression because of the baseball style cap he's wearing.

"Alright," he says.

I place both my hands on his shoulders and the electricity that shoots through me almost pushes me off balance. I think he feels it too because he looks up when my hands are holding on to him. His expression is one I can't figure out, but I swallow nervously and raise my leg slowly. He slides the band up my calf with his fingers and takes advantage by sliding both hands slowly up my leg and stops mid-thigh, adjusting the band.

"Like that?" he asks. I'm looking down, hoping my wet pussy doesn't drip down my thighs, and he realizes how aroused I am by his hands on my skin.

"Higher, please," I say. God, I want him to keep touching me.

"Are you sure?" I nod *yes*, holding on to him as his muscles bunch under my hands and my pussy gets wetter. I almost close my eyes as my heart beats wildly. His hands are back on the band, and he hooks his finger underneath, sliding it up higher. He uses the inside of my thigh to raise it higher, using the other hand to assist. His fingers brush the side of my panties, and he can briefly feel the folds of my pussy and how drenched my lace panties are under my little red skirt.

He can smell my arousal because his nostrils flair slightly, inhaling my scent. When finished, I place my leg back down and release my hold on his shoulder, missing the touch of his muscles underneath my hands. I would love to feel his body and what it would feel like to be in his arms. He springs from his chair and I can hear one guy in the back shouting, "Get it, champ!" Ignoring him, I look up at Nate. He is so much taller than me, even in these heels.

He leans into me close and whispers in my ear, "Your pussy is so wet for me and only me, isn't it?" I look up at him and motion for him to lean down so I can whisper back.

"Yes," I say. I place my hands on his chest and he makes no move to remove them.

Looking down at my hands, I lift them, and surprisingly, he holds my hands in place and leans into my ear, "I want you," he breathes. He looks down at me, his gaze intense. "I want us to start over." He holds out his hand. "I'm Nate."

Looking at his outstretched hand, I slide my soft one into his. "I'm Giselle." His hand squeezes gently with promise.

The manager, Linda, comes and breaks the spell he had me in. "Money Monroe," she calls out to me. I look up and step back, putting distance between me and Nate, my hand falling. I turn around.

"Yes," I say, looking at her.

"I need to see you in my office." I can still feel his heat behind me.

"It's okay. Go," he says. I follow her as Nate sits back down at his table, watching me, as I walk toward Linda's office. Once inside, she closes the door. I stand motionless, wondering what I did wrong, and if it's because of my behavior with Nate.

I don't know what came over me, letting him touch me and admitting that I wanted him and only him. I still have his scent mixed with his cologne intoxicating my senses, making my thighs clench in want.

"I have a proposition for you that was requested this morning." I frown in confusion.

"What proposition?" I ask.

She slides the paper forward on her desk. "This is an NDA if you agree. It outlines the terms of the agreement to take place this weekend." I take the paper and read the name of the person requesting with my full name at the top.

Scanning the document, she continues as I stare at the name in shock. "You have obviously caught the attention of Nate 'The Reaper' Phoenix, Pro MMA fighter. He would like to request a personal dance at his home, just the two of you. I have let Mr. Phoenix know that your role here at the club is to choreograph and dance. He knows you do not take your clothes off or give any special services." I look at the paper and see that he wants me to dance for him with no penetration, but only wearing a thong. I can choose the clothing, song, etc...

"I see that it's for the weekend and that I leave Saturday and arrive back Sunday evening. Will this interrupt my job here?" She smiles.

"Honey, he is paying you 25,000 dollars for your time." My eyes go wide at the large amount to just dance for one guy, but not just any guy. The one guy who makes me feel hot and wet all over. I have never thought about having sex so much since laying my eyes on him. When he touches me, I'm lost in his spell and everything fades away; the club, the music, the people, all that is left his him and I suspended in a world of lust. I think about it and weigh my options. Dance for a crowd or for just one man who wants to enjoy watching me? Paying more money than I make in year. I figured my goal in dancing is to save up for my very own dance academy. I have thought about it since I came back home. Dancing is what I love, and it's the only thing I have ever wanted. A man just takes what he wants, and when he's done with you, casts you aside as though you mean nothing but a good time. That much I have learned about being here. Men married, and not married, frequently coming to the club knowing some of the famous athletes have long-term steady girlfriends. It doesn't stop them from paying for extra favors in the back room. What would it matter if it's someone I actually find an attractive on a sexual level? He can easily come in here and watch me dance, just not topless, but some outfits I thought of wearing on some nights are borderline from being just that, practically naked, that leaves little to the imagination.

With my decision made, I look up. "Do you have a pen?"

She smiles. "I am glad you are accepting the most generous offer I have ever seen in a club I have managed. Just one thing, Giselle, be careful with him. I saw the way he looks at you and I have seen that look before."

"What do you mean?"

"Sweetheart, that man looks at you like you are the last cup of water in a desert, and he is dying of thirst," she chuckles. I nervously sign the papers, knowing I cannot let anyone know about the agreement or give any information regarding the arrangement.

* * *

The next morning, Brie and I head to the diner for our morning shift. I tell her about the agreement, even if I signed the NDA. Like I wouldn't tell Brie some MMA fighter who could kill me with one punch is taking me to his house in Las Vegas to do a striptease, ending in just my thong.

"Are you fucking kidding me, Giselle?" she says, smiling.

"Yeah. I actually signed the NDA and agreed to dance for him. I am so nervous. What if he is a creep and I go missing?"

"No way. I don't believe he's a creep. He likes to be alone and hates clingy women. Probably why he hired you. When he has his little tryst, it is widely known he leaves a care package with designer purses and perfumes that cost thousands for every woman he takes to bed and leaves afterward. There was, like, an entire article about him regarding his love life and all the women who throw themselves at him, and the ones who are lucky enough to have had sex."

"I guess that's a relief. He will be bored with me and leave me alone. It states no penetration, so he isn't interested in me like that. Just a lap dance and minimal clothing that no one will see me doing."

"Exactly, Giselle. He is paying you a lot for just that. Do you know how many men Diamond and Treasure have to see in that back room to make that kind of cash? He could have easily just offered you the money for sex."

"I get it, Brie. It would be dumb to pass it up and I definitely need the money. I would have turned it down if he had requested more. Anyway, I get the key to the apartment today and need to go to the furniture store to at least buy a bed," I say excitedly.

"I know! I am happy for you, Giselle. And the added bonus that you are just one floor down from me and we can hang out and have movie nights!"

5
GISELLE

We arrive and park her car in front of the diner. The next thing I have to get is a car, unless I walk. Uber is not very popular in smaller towns and I feel bad asking Brie for a ride everywhere I go. We get out in our makeshift pink uniforms that are mid-thigh, but on Brie and me, they look like a server waiting to seduce the customer for how form-fitting they are on our toned bodies. I put my name tag on and pick up my wavy hair in a messy bun with some loose tendrils of hair framing my face. I'm wearing pink lip-gloss, eyeliner and some blush to look presentable. I have only had five hours of sleep from the previous night dancing at The Porcelain Dollhouse.

When we scan the parking lot, we notice expensive cars, an Escalade, Raptor, Merc, and even a Ferrari at the diner. Great, must be the customers from the club, trying to break a hangover. We walk through the back door and Joe greets us both.

"Thank God you girls are here," he says.

"Hi Joe," we say in unison, smiling.

"Please help with the four booths, one through four out front," he says, sighing. He seems overwhelmed and exhausted.

"On it, Joe," Brie says.

"Don't you worry about a thing, Joe. Brie showed me everything there is to know, and I have memorized the menu," I tell him as he smiles.

"I knew you girls were too smart. I'm lucky to have you helping an old man out."

We grab a pen, order pad, and head out to take the orders before customers start to complain. I reach the first booth and stop. So does Brie when we spot Jace and Jason sitting, scanning the menu. Brie notices and places her hand on my arm.

"Don't worry. We can handle it," I whisper so no one can hear me. I can hear her nervous exhale.

"Okay," she whispers back. I walk up to them, and Brie starts on the second booth of men. You can see they all play for the Ravens and are here together.

They both look up and Jace, as always, with is snarky comments says, "Well, well. Look who's here and works at the diner. You girls are very busy." He looks back at Brie, acknowledging us both. Jason drops the menu and looks surprised to see me standing in front of him, waiting.

"What can we get you?" I ask, trying to ignore his comments. He smiles and the guys in the booth are waiting for him to continue.

"How about letting Jason and I take you and Brie out tonight?" he says.

My face gets serious, and I look at both of them. "No, thank you. Are you going to order, or I can take the next table down until you decide?" I ask.

Jason looks up with hopeful eyes. "I'm sorry about Jace. He just isn't good at expressing himself," he says.

I look at him with a straight face. "Then you should keep better company because he's a total jerk."

Jason elbows Jace to stop. "Look, we're sorry for everything that happened before. I want to just say one thing and I will order."

I tap my foot, waiting with an eyebrow raised. "Okay. What is it?" I ask. Brie stops writing the other guy's orders and listens. The diner kind of got quieter, probably people rubber necking to see what is going on over here. I have my back turned to the other two booths, so I can't see for sure if they are listening.

"Remember the last time we went horseback riding on your favorite two horses, and we stopped by the tree at your parents' farm?" I frown at the memory of the most beautiful horses my father had on the farm. The sadness clearly written on my face as he looks at me. Unshed tears instantly fill my eyes as the memory of my childhood home being sold to the highest bidder to pay off all the creditors my parents owed. He notices my instant sadness and inhales deeply. He continues as I stay silent, "I want to let you know that I have never forgotten that day. That part was genuine and I'm sorry if you thought for one second it wasn't. I am also sorry about your loss. If there is anything you ever need, I will be there for you Giselle, always."

I look into his handsome face, into his green eyes, and I see the sincerity there, the honesty in his words. When I was a teenager yearning for a first love, hoping to find it, he never said the words that a girl longs to hear. He let me think all this time that my first kiss was a joke, a mistake. I cried myself to sleep that night, feeling unwanted and undesired by a boy I found attractive. I stay silent as he looks at me and his eyes soften. He looks older than when I last saw him, but in a more attractive way; not a boy, but a very attractive man with a nice body that can fill out a T-shirt like it's no one's business. It's a shame to think he kissed me for a fifty-dollar bet. It was a long time ago.

"Okay. So, what can I get you both?" I feigned indifference because it's the only armor I possess. He smiles, knowing I believe him.

"Can we get the traditional breakfast and orange juice?" he asks. I write it down.

"It will be out shortly." I turn to leave and notice Brie is taking the order of the third booth and I slow down as I noticed who is sitting in the fourth booth with his manager, Nate "The Reaper" Phoenix. He looks up and down at me in my uniform with a smirk. Great.

I walk up to the table and repeat the same, "What can I get you both?" I ask. Nate looks at my name tag and then at my face. Probably noticing I gave him my real name, or maybe I look different in a uniform.

I look at his manager. He smiles. "Hello, my name is Jaden, and you already met Nate. He's a big deal in MMA."

"Hi," I say. I smile, but he notices it doesn't quite reach my eyes. I look over at Nate, including him in what I'm about to say. He looks at me and then looks away, staring at Jaden. "I'm sorry, but I don't quite follow your sport and I honestly didn't know your name until someone mentioned it." I can see Nate stiffen a bit that I didn't recognize him like he is used to.

"So, you never knew who he was when you were waiting for us at the club?" Jaden asks.

"Nope." I smile.

"Interesting." He grins.

"So, what can I get you boys?" I look at Nate while he looks at his phone.

He looks up and says with a smile, "I already have a date with you, so we would like to add five scrambled eggs, and a water, please." I look at Jaden and he grins as Brie walks up next to me.

"Everything okay here, Giselle?" Brie asks.

Jaden speaks up before I get to tell her everything is fine. "Everything is fine, especially now that you're here, beautiful." I look at Brie as her cheeks blush pink, but she quickly composes herself.

"Okay. Well, let me help you get the food for Jace and Jason over there before Jace starts with his shit," she says, leaving to the back to get them their orders. Jaden and Nate look over their way with a glare.

"How do you know them?" Nate asks as he looks at me with his gorgeous face and black hoodie.

"Brie and Jace used to date back in high school, and Jason always hung out with Jace, and Brie is my best friend. We all lived in the same town close to here before they went pro," I say.

"So how come the Ravens starting tight end, Jason Bresely, speaks to you like you were his girl?" Nate asks. I look at him, not understanding why he wants to know.

"I honestly don't know. We were friends and he would come over to my house and hang out, but that's it. I told you before, I'm no one's girl, and if you want to eat, I have to put your order in." Avoiding the subject from his interrogation about Jason and Jace, I'm trying to figure out what his problem is. I see Brie, good on her word, brought out the food out for the guys in booth one and two, so I help her with the third booth, and put in Nate and Jaden's order. Joe looks at me with a twinkle in his eye when I'm at the back preparing the tray to bring the food and silverware out.

"Looks like you and Brie have the attention of all the star athletes out there," he says.

"Yeah, and none of them are worth a girl's heartbreak over, believe me. They don't have good intentions, they're all the same."

Joe chuckles. "Come now, Giselle, you know Jason likes you and has always had an eye for you. I think he has honestly liked you since you were teenagers."

"Yeah, was that before or after he took a bet to kiss me for fifty bucks?" His eyes widen.

"What is wrong with that boy? Let me guess, he played it off."

"You got it, Joe. Brie and I are just jokes and a nice laugh at our expense. Nothing special."

He stops what he is doing and looks at me. "Boys do stupid things sometimes when they really like a girl and don't know how to approach her without hurting them. Look at Jace and Brie. Jace has been in love with Brie since he was a kid, and he just can't deal with the fact of who her mother is, and how people will judge them. It's cowardly, but all the same, it's what everyone knows is the problem." Joe would know this, being from a small town, where everyone is in everyone's businesses.

"I guess, but we shouldn't judge people or use them. It's unfair," I say. I look at where Jace and Jason are sitting and realize Jace is looking at Brie as she takes an order from another customer on the other side. He can't stop staring at her while she isn't looking, and when I look at Jason, he is staring right at me with a grin, and soft eyes. I look away and notice the guys in the back with cold, hard glares aimed right at Jace and Jason. Feeling the tension, I head to pick up Nate and Jaden's order, the sound of the bell from the cook signaling that their food is ready to be taken to their table.

I place the food on the tray and head over to them, placing their breakfast in front of them. "Is there anything else I can get you guys?"

"How come you and your friend work here when you work at the club?" Jaden asks. It's a stupid question that I find annoying.

"Why do people work? Because they obviously need the money?" I say sarcastically.

"I set myself up for that one, didn't I?"

Jace interrupts and speaks up loudly to get my attention. "Hey, sweetheart. Can you stop the small talk and come over here so we can pay?" I inwardly sigh and roll my eyes. Nate gets up and stands behind me as I look at Jace.

"Hey dickhead, why don't you shut the fuck up and wait. We're not done talking. When we're done and I decide to let her go over there so you can pay, she will let you know." My heart races as I feel the rage radiating from him, behind me.

Jace gives him a murderous glare. "You got a problem with me champ?" Jace says.

"Yeah, I actually do. You're fucking up my breakfast and my time. So just shut the fuck up and wait," Nate says while Jaden chuckles.

Brie breaks the tension, "It's okay guys, chill. Jace, here is the bill." She grabs it and sets on their table and gives me a smile, while Nate sits back down. Jaden looks pissed and gets up to go over to Brie. She looks surprised when she sees him coming over her way. He stands next to her and whispers in her ear. Her eyes widen and she nods. He hands her a piece of paper, and he walks back to the booth with a grin on his face. Nate shakes his head, not believing him.

"What?" Jaden says.

"Nothing," Nate says. I walk over so I can collect the payment from Jace and Jason's table.

Jason's hand brushes mine as I pick up the money, noticing there are too many bills. I frown, looking at a thousand dollars in tip. "We can't accept this," I whisper, looking up at him. "Please take it."

"We can't. It's not right and feels wrong." I can't believe they want to tip Brie and me this much money. I don't want to feel that we owe them anything because we accepted a big tip. He gets up from the booth as Jace walks out, looking down at me because of his height as I step back.

"I overheard you needing the money and why you work here. If it was up to me, you wouldn't work at these places, and I figure the more you make, the less you have to work, especially over there." His words are above a whisper, and I can smell his spicy cologne. I never expected him to say that. "I'll see you later, beautiful," he says as he walks out of the diner. I turn around and see Brie gaping at me as I give her the other half of the money. She looks at the amount of money and her eyes go wide, just like mine did.

We go about working in the diner, serving the rest of the customers. Then, Nate gives the signal that he is ready for me to come over. I head over to their table, and he has this unreadable look on his face I can't figure out, while Jaden stays silent.

"Ready?" I ask. I clear their table and leave them the bill. He doesn't even flip the paper over to see how much it is. He reaches inside his pocket as I place the dirty dishes in the bin for the dishwasher to clean. When I turn around, they're both gone, left without saying goodbye. I feel disappointed as walk over to the table, and see a roll of hundreds. I count them and there is ten thousand dollars in total with a note on the bill. The money for the bill is also there, with a note written in his handwriting. It reads *Five thousand for Brie and five thousand for Giselle... See you soon, Beautiful.*

I take the bill with the note and tell Brie. She puts her hand over her mouth. "Holy shit," she whispers.

"I know," I say. She shows me the note Jaden gave her showing is phone number. I grin at her and giggle.

6

GISELLE

The next day, I look online and order a bed and some kitchen essentials because I'm too exhausted from work. I was left with nothing from my childhood home, having nowhere to put it, and having to sell as much as I could. I have to sleep at Brie's until my bed arrives, but at least it will be fun to have a girls sleepover.

"So, are you still nervous about this weekend?" Brie asks.

I inwardly sigh. "Yeah, of course. I'm going to his house alone and dancing for his eyes only. I'm nervous and he is obviously counting on me showing up."

"I think he really has a thing for you."

"Maybe, or he just wants someone who is paid to do what he wants. I really don't know. Let's see what happens," I say.

"I also noticed Jason definitely has a thing for you. He was referencing the kiss, wasn't he?"

"Yeah, he was coming clean after all this time, but that ship sailed a long time ago."

It's Friday night and the club is getting more and more popular for the customers to frequent. I see Jake listening to his playlist that he will mix tonight. I tap his shoulder, waiting for him to take his headphones off.

"Hey, I have a song for my solo tonight."

"Really?" he asks. Jake is handsome with green eyes, and is a very talented DJ from London. He appreciates dance and music and we have that much in common in a friendly way.

"When I'm up, can you play *In My Feelings* by Lana, please?"

He looks at me with his eyebrows raised. "Sure, beautiful. That kind of night huh?"

"Yeah," I say. If he only knew that tomorrow I had to stroke the lion in his lair. "Thank you, Jake, you're the best."

"Anything for you, sweetness." I give him a hug and get ready, changing into my outfit for the night. I am heading home early to get ready for Saturday. A car will pick me up to take the flight to Vegas and I will have a car waiting for me to take me to Nate, all outlined in the contract I signed.

The club is at capacity tonight, and the energy is electrifying. Our tables are full, Nate and Jaden seated at the usual table. I also see Jace and Jason with his boys from the Ravens, watching them throw money to Treasure and Diamond dancing on the stage. Brie and I take their orders and they order the same, watching the show, but waiting. Nate doesn't look at me and Jaden is the only one ordering and interacting with Brie. From the corner of my eye, I can see Jason tracking my every movement. I make my way around the club in my lace thigh-high pantyhose and garters, my bra, and booty shorts with rhinestones shimmering in the lights moving to the rhythm of the music. I decide on a black tutu and black ballet slippers for my solo tonight. Something different and sexual to go with my choice of music in the background. I check the time, Jake will call me up any second now.

"Money Monroe! Where are you, beautiful?" Jake speaks over the mic. I look up between the tables next to Treasure and Diamond, making my way to the back. I raise my hand, the light shining on me as everyone looks over. "You have a special request, sweetheart."

Great, when I think it's an easy night, I get a special request. A special request is someone requesting to walk in front of the stage, some give money, flowers, and gifts. You must accept, by company policy; the tips are yours to keep, any tips that are thrown on stage to the girls that were on shift that night is dispersed evenly. Guys love to do that to their favorites who come on stage. I wonder who it is. I look around and spot Nate, and he is not even looking my way, he's looking at Jason with a death glare. Whatever, I have to get on stage to start my solo and can't think about it right now, whoever it is, I am going to find out, it's probably some guy that has come in and has a crush. Brie tells me it happens all the time.

"Welcome to the stage, the beautiful and talented Miss Money Monroe! Make it rain!" Jake says, echoing through the club as Lana Del Rey plays.

I make it on stage in my tutu, walking on pointe in ballerina slippers.

Yeah, a ballerina performing in a strip club. Like I could make that shit up...

7

GISELLE

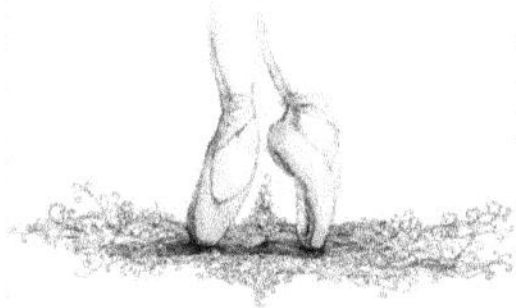

I tip toe on ballerina slippers, feeling Lana's voice over my body and I twist my leg up and look back. I continue to dance and grab the stripper pole, fly around in circles, holding myself suspended in the air, with my legs pointed. All the guys from the football ball team are looking in awe, standing and cheering, as I suspend myself in my slippers with my legs straight. Moving from one stripper pole to the other, I twirl around in circles, and land. I have my hair in a messy bun, and I twirl in my ballerina slippers in circles as fast I can, watching the rhinestones glittering like blinding lights until the song ends. I wait for the person who made the special request to show.

I find Jason with a bouquet of red roses, and something in his hand I can't see. I walk up as far as I can go, the stage has a bar in the way so that people can't just go up on stage and touch the girls performing. Chris, securing the area, is watching Jason warily, making sure he doesn't cross the line. I stand there in my slippers and tutu, and he comes forward, handing me the flowers, and my eyes soften. I have never received roses before. His friends whistle and I watch as he removes what appears to be two tickets with lots of money. He places the little stacks, making sure they don't fall in my garters, band of my tutu, bra straps and I suddenly find myself full of hundred-dollar bills. I bend down and he whispers, "Please be there, beautiful." I frown, slightly confused. He kisses me on the cheek and for the life of me, I let him.

I suddenly feel intense eyes on me that feel as though they could set this place on fire. I look over at Nate and he is glaring with his fist clenched tight with a murderous look I have ever seen, aimed right at me. Suddenly, I pull back and stand up straight, nervous. I look at Jason and he is unaware of what is going on behind him, looking at me intently, he abruptly turns around and walks back to his table. Nate is standing, breathing fast, like he is about to lose his shit. I turn around and go back to the dressing room where I find Brie.

"Holy shit, Giselle! You have hundred-dollar bills everywhere. What are the tickets for?" she asks.

"I-I-I don't know!" I say breathlessly. I pull them out from my garter, and they are indeed two tickets to the next Ravens game the following Monday night. That's what he meant when he said he hoped to see me there. We count the money and it's exactly twenty thousand dollars. I can't believe Jason would give me so much money.

"I told you," Brie says as she winks. Her solo we practiced is up next, and when she returns, she has the same amount of money, minus the tickets from Jace.

"Jaden didn't look thrilled. Nate had to hold him back," Brie says as I wait for her to end the night. I feel this could be a problem if they don't put a stop to it and soon, but we have done nothing wrong.

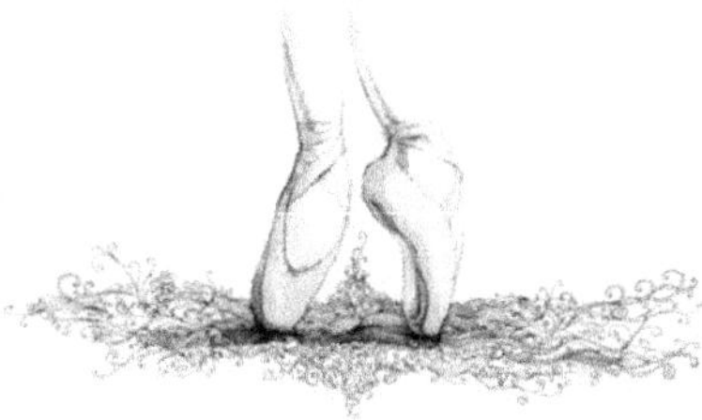

Saturday morning comes, and the car is waiting for me. It's a black Escalade, and a door opens for me and I see Nate in the backseat. I take the captain's chair to the left with my small gym bag. He has his hoodie over his head, and he appears to be asleep. He says nothing, and neither does Jaden as the car drives out onto the highway. I stay silent and decide to listen to music, Lana Del Rey playing on my playlist, as we reach the airstrip that has a private plane ready to take us to Vegas.

I sit on the plane, and I am offered something to drink. I opt for water, leaving the headphones in, as it is my only sanity to calm my nervousness. Jake sent me a playlist to create some dances for my next solo. I find the song and listen to the beat, concentrating when I feel a tap on my shoulder. I look over and Nate is talking to me, but I can't make out the words. I take my headphones off.

"What?" I ask.

"We're here. Let's go," he says. Embarrassed, I get up and grab my bag close to my chest, wearing sweats, and a leotard with sneakers.

I let my hair down, cascading in waves around my face and down my back. I walk down the steps to an awaiting car I have never seen. It's like those supercars you see on TV, just different. Nate opens the door and I slide inside. He closes the door and he gets in, revving the engine. He takes off toward his house while Jaden and the other people in his entourage leave in blacked out SUVs.

We arrive by the time the sun is setting, at the most beautiful, white, modern house, overlooking the skyline. The gates open automatically and the car roars forward. He parks in front of the most impressive house I have ever seen, with manicured lawns. He opens the door and holds his hand for me to take it, helping me out of the car. I follow him in to the house the most expensive designer must have designed, with no traces that someone actually lives here. It's beautiful, but impersonal and lacks warmth. He shows me to a guest room with an en suite bathroom.

"You can change in here and it's where you can sleep after, 'til morning. A car will take you back to the airport," he says.

"Okay," is all I say. I'm so nervous I hope he can't see my heart beating out of my chest. He walks me to the family room where there is surround sound where I can play my music, and a white couch that looks like a bunch of clouds. He dims the lights, giving a soft glow to the room, while the sun sets.

"Your home is beautiful," I say. He looks at me and dismisses my compliment.

"I will see you here in 30 minutes."

"Yes, of course," I say.

Turning around quickly, I leave toward the room he said I could use, feeling embarrassed. He probably thinks I am one of those girls that only cares about wealth and trying to snag a rich guy. I freshen up in the bathroom that has the most beautiful soaps and lotions, touching nothing. I want nothing he leaves here for me. He is paying me to dance and that's it. The sooner I dance, the sooner I can go back home.

I decide to play *High by the Beach* by Lana as my song of choice, get changed into a lace bra, thong, pairing it with high black heels, and thigh highs with garter hooks. I place a satin bow tied to my lower back, right above my tail bone. I wear a robe to walk through his massive house, not giving away what I'm wearing, as I walk toward the living room.

I reach the family room and he is sitting with a pair of grey sweats and no shirt on. I look at his muscled chest and flat stomach showing his tattoos, and my pussy floods in my lace thong. His legs are stretched out, waiting for me. I look at his face and his hazel eyes are hungry when they look at me. I decided to wear light makeup, since I have to dance on his lap, finishing the touch by spraying my favorite perfume my mother gifted me when I turned fifteen, by Jo Malone.

His eyes never leave my face and body as I move to play the music on my phone. When I'm ready, I steady my breath as I untie my robe and let it slide down to the floor.

I hear his intake of breath right before the song begins and I turn around, revealing my bow as I bend over so he can see my ass with the imprint of my pussy through the thong. I bring myself up, walk toward him, and straddle his lap on the couch. He looks at me, unties the bow, and lets it fall. I spread my hands on his chest, caressing his skin, and beautiful body. Feeling the grooves of his carved muscles, enjoying the warmth his skin provides.

He looks down to where the outline of my pussy is on his hard cock as he slides his fingers on the band of my thong. I begin to move in circles to the lyrics of the song, and his dick is rock hard. My pussy gets so wet and I moan as he slides his hands up my stomach slowly to my back, undoing my bra. When my breasts are standing taught, he places his face to my tits and takes a nipple in his mouth and my head falls back, holding his face in place.

"Fuck," he hisses. He lets go of one nipple, sucking with just enough pressure that it doesn't hurt, and tends to the other. I lean my face to his and he takes my lips. He kisses me, devouring my mouth as he sucks and twirls his tongue. He is breathless when he releases my mouth for me to breathe.

"Fuck, I want you. You're so beautiful and you feel so damn good." I smile and kiss him again. I want to feel his tongue and I love the way his dick feels rubbing on my pussy through the lace thong. He keeps sucking and kissing my lips while when he slides a finger to feel my wet pussy. He dips his finger inside my folds, and I freeze like a bucket of cold water, realizing this is not how I want to have sex, being paid for a dance, like a paid escort. He feels my body go rigid.

"Stop, please," I say, out of breath. He's any woman's dream; attractive, with the feel of a massive cock that promises all the pleasure a girl could dream of. He tastes and smells like heaven, all masculine and hard, with a face that should go on the cover of a magazine.

I whisper next to his ear, "Not like this, please stop," I say as the song ends. I get up off of him, holding my breasts with one arm, and try to pick up my robe and bra with the satin bow from his family room floor. I run out the room without so much as a backward glance and reach the guest room with tears in my eyes because of how much I wanted him to take me right there on his couch. To feel him inside me when I know he sees me as a girl who was hired to dance for his pleasure, meaning nothing to him. I am so confused that I want him this badly, almost giving in, and letting him have me. I fall asleep, lost in my feelings, alone in a bed, at a house I'm unfamiliar with, tears streaming down my face, and wishing my parents were still alive.

I wake up to a noise hitting something over and over. I quickly shower to not miss the car that will take me to the airport so I can go home. When I get out of the shower, I can still hear the noise. I make my way through the house toward the sound as it gets louder. I drop my bag off at the door, continuing to hear it. Hitting over and over... I suddenly walk into a side of the house that looks like a huge gym with what must be a punching bag.

I walk inside the gym and can see Nate hitting the bag with

multiple combinations over and over like a machine with sweat dripping down his beautiful body muscles as he moves. He senses my presence as he turns toward the entrance where I'm standing. He drops his arms from his fighter's stance and looks at me.

"What?" he asks. I stiffen and feel bad for interrupting him, and his training.

"I'm sorry. I was just leaving and wanted to say goodbye."

"Okay. Bye," he says sarcastically. I turn to go, and he stops me. "There is something for you on the kitchen island."

"Okay. Thank you." I give him a fake smile and turn to leave. The car must be waiting outside already, so I quickly make my way to the kitchen island, and stop dead. I see the famous bag everyone talks about, the care package with all the designer items he gives to the girls that run through his life. I look at it, like it holds the body of a dead corpse. I see a pen in the corner by the refrigerator and quickly find a napkin to write a note, placing it next to the bag, as I leave out the door of his cold house to an awaiting car.

8

NATE

I can't believe I did that when she was dancing on my lap. I didn't mean for it to get that far. I have been hitting the bag all night, punishing myself for going too far with her. She must think I wanted to pay her for sex and froze on me like I was the most disgusting thing to touch her perfect body. She is the most beautiful woman I have ever put my hands on. She's so soft and smells like heaven. Her pussy was so wet on my dick as she straddled my lap, dancing to the music. I almost lost it. I wanted to lay her on my couch and sink my cock in her just to watching her come undone in my arms. Her lips tasted soft like sweet candy, her arousal for me was even sweeter, and I was dying to taste her. If she only knew how much I wanted that sweet pussy in my mouth, to watch her come, screaming my name over and over.

I should have been nicer to her before she left. I was an asshole, not even asking if she wanted a glass of water, but I couldn't sleep hoping she wouldn't hear me having my nightmares.

I wanted to kill that asshole for giving her the flowers and money in front of everyone. Now I just proved to her that the asshole is really me. His little friend also did the same to get a rise out of Jaden, both of them knowing I can't lose my shit before my next fight. They think they one-upped us. They have another thing coming. One thing I have is the media all over me, and I will make sure they see who got the cream in front of everyone.

As for Giselle, I'm not sure how I am going to fix it between us, but make no mistake, I will have her in my bed. I felt the want and need for her. She wants to fight what she feels, and I'm holding back. I just don't know how to get her to see me. It's the first time a woman as denied me.

When I see her dance, transfixed by how beautiful she moves with the music, I can honestly say, I could sit there and watch her forever. When I saw her with the ballet slippers, my dick was so hard looking at her, making love to the music with her body, unconsciously I was wishing it was me. I have never wanted someone like her. I acted like a total idiot. I will lose her interest if I don't figure something out quickly.

I keep hitting the bag, exhausted from holding myself back, from wanting to walk in the bedroom and take what I want.

"What the fuck is wrong with me?" I mutter.

I walk out to the kitchen to get a glass of water and I stop when I look at the bag I told her was hers to keep. The dubbed care package I give all the girls I fuck, even though technically she denied me from fucking her last night. I wonder what she meant when she said, "Not like this." Seeing there is a note in front of the bag, I want to kick myself for being a total dick, dismissing her like she was a pest. I pick up the napkin written in her handwriting.

I'm not interested. Leave it for the next girl.

I throw the glass of water at the sink, water and shards of glass fly everywhere. I know I've fucked up.

9

GISELLE

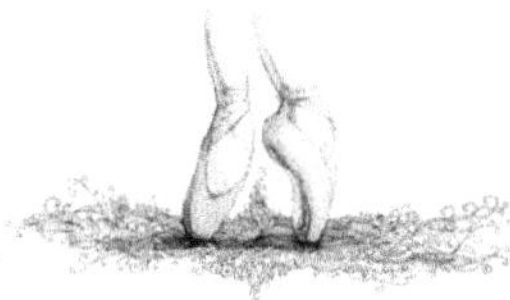

I arrive in Sioux Falls and tell Brie everything that happened through tears. She comforts me by rubbing my back.

"Forget about him, Giselle. He doesn't deserve you. He's obviously twisted and has some serious baggage," she says. "You may have lost your parents, but you are dancing and not screwing anyone for money. You agreed because you're attracted to him and what woman wouldn't want to spend the night with Nate?"

I need stop feeling sorry for myself, maybe she's right. He's just not for me and probably regrets having me over. It's probably why he acted the way he did in the morning.

The week passes by quickly, and then it's Friday. Brie and I have made plans to go to the football game on Monday. I say, what the heck? It's not like we're going with them, it's just to watch them play. Anyone would die for those tickets. They are right behind the players at the stadium. I tell Jake about the song he sent me, selecting his mixed version of *Absurd* by Fluke. Getting ready with the black light glow paint and neon lights, I decide I'm going to complete the look with a Tron movie vibe and wear a white wig, swinging laser beams glowing in the reflection of the mirrors and black lights. I think it will look badass in the vast warehouse of the club.

When the club opens its doors, there's not an empty seat in the house. Saturdays are getting like that as well. I don't get to the VIP tables as I need extra time to prepare for my solo and the manager said it was fine. I would mix another song, *Sweet Dreams* by Trinix, making it an entire performance to mix it up here since we have familiar faces.

I look out toward the DJ booth at Jake and he signals to me that he will call me out soon. I scan the crowd and I'm surprised to see Jaden and Nate, waiting for Brie. He hasn't seen me, and I want to keep it that way.

"Hey girl," Diamond startles me.

"Oh my God, Diamond, my heart just jumped out of my chest."

"Are you nervous about the fighter looking for you?"

"What do you mean, looking for me?" I ask.

"Yeah, I overhead him asking Brie for you while his manager is trying to get in Brie's good graces. She's giving him the professional server treatment."

"I'm just nervous as hell and now I just saw Jace and Jason walk in."

"Here." She gives me a shot of what appears to be tequila. I drink the shot back, coughing as it lights my throat on fire, giving me liquid courage.

"Thank you, Diamond."

"Don't sweat it. You got this. Dance on him, that will get him to chill the fuck out if front of everyone. Let's see what he does."

I get ready while the alcohol loosens me up and Jake announces my name. I decide to take her advice and do something crazy. The song by Fluke begins and the neon lights take control while I twirl, and the black lights reflect the glow paint. I dance behind the pole and the song picks up. Everyone is freaking out because of the lights, making it seem like I'm everywhere. Some start to dance to the beat. I spin the lights, and the paint I'm holding goes down my body, dripping between my breasts, glowing in the dark. Catcalls can be heard as I walk toward Nate and his eyebrow raises as I straddle him and do the same moves I did on his couch. I'm facing him and he looks at me as I grind on his dick through his pants. I'm wearing shiny black boots that give me the advantage of dancing better.

"What are you going to do with that, champ?" a guy shouts to my right as the song switches to *Sweet Dreams*. Nate's hands slide down, over my body, touching my breasts. I hold his face to my chest, he looks at me while I slowly slide down back to sit on his lap.

He grabs my chin and lightly kisses me on my lips and the crowd goes wild. I quickly get up and go back to the pole and dance, twirling on it to finish the song, holding in the excitement that I let him kiss me.

His kiss lights a fire in me that I can't put out. I never expected him to touch me or kiss me in front of everyone. Diamond was right, seeing what he would do. And I loved his hands on me, setting my body on my fire, building a pressure between my legs that only he can release. I change and head out to meet Brie to help her with the tables. She smiles at me as I meet up with her in my fishnets and booty shorts, opting for a tank top instead of just the bra. I see her watch go off, indicating Nate and Jaden's table needs assistance. I make my way over as Nate looks at me with hunger and desire.

I get to the table and I am about to ask what they need, but Nate speaks up, "Leave with me tonight?"

"Excuse me?"

"Leave with me and I will have you back on Sunday. Stay the weekend with me, please?"

"I can't, I have work," I say.

"Take the weekend off. You and Brie can come with us. We

have a charity event, and we want you girls to go. We are asking you girls out, officially." He grins.

"We accept," Brie chimes in. I look at her and my eyes go wide. "When do we leave so I can have her ready?" .

"Tonight. We came hoping you would say yes."

"So, you came all the way over here to ask us if we would go out with you guys?" I ask.

"Yeah, I don't have your phone number, do I?"

"You never asked for it," I tell Nate.

"Well, now that you mention it, I want it," he says, his hazel eyes challenging me to deny him.

"Okay." I pull out my phone from my bra and hand it to him. He smirks, seeing where I keep it.

"Interesting place to keep your phone."

"Everywhere else you can notice it," I say, jokingly. He looks me up and down and then enters his contact info into my phone. He grabs his and sends me a text.

"Now I have yours and you have mine. If there is anything you ever need, you call me."

I smile and look at the text he sent me and contact name he entered:

Giselle's lover: I can't wait to taste you.

I look at him and goosebumps break out all over my arms when his fingers brush mine as he handed mc thc phone.

"We will be ready in fifteen minutes, but we need to go home and get clothes."

"Nah, don't worry about that. We need to go shopping, anyway," he says. Jaden is listening and smiling at Brie.

"Okay. If you say so," I say.

We leave at the end of our shift, requesting tomorrow and Sunday off. Leaving for the airport in a Black Merc, we arrive to board the private plane. They offer Brie and I champagne as the plane takes off. We are both nervous at the realization of our impulsivity, and we just take the flutes of champagne handed to us and drink in the sweet taste of alcohol. I never drink, but tonight, I make an exception. I make sure to not lose my head with alcohol, but just enough to relax. When they offer us more, we respectfully decline. Nate sits next to me and twirls my hair around his finger while watching Jaden and Brie in conversation.

"I'm sorry about the other day. I'm grumpy in the morning. I couldn't sleep and I feel bad for treating you like crap," he says.

I am surprised by his apology, but at least he's capable of recognizing when he treats someone like dirt. I decide to accept his apology. He didn't force me to do anything I didn't want. He left me alone when I bolted and I figured I was also to blame for allowing him to go further. I just didn't think it was right, the agreement was just to dance. "Okay. I accept your apology on one condition."

"Name it."

I look into his beautiful face with his small straight nose and sexy lips. "Don't give me one of those bags," I laugh.

He looks up and puts a hand over his face. "Yeah, I get it. That was in poor taste. Deal. No gift bags."

We stay watching each other until I close my eyes and sleep for the next hour. I realize I fell asleep on his chest with his hands in my hair. When the plane lands, he gently wakes me from the most blissful sleep. He holds my hand as Jaden guides Brie. She gives me a knowing smile as they take us to Nate's house. When we arrive, Brie's mouth hangs open as she takes in the grandeur of his house. Jaden takes her to the other side of the house while Nate guides me to his master bedroom. I admire the crisp white sheets on his king-sized bed overlooking the pool through the french doors. The doors are open, letting the breeze from the night into the bedroom.

"Your bedroom is beautiful," I say.

"It's more beautiful when you're in it." I smile at his attempt to flatter me. "The bathroom is in there." He grabs a white T-shirt so I can change, since I don't have any clothes to sleep in. Grabbing his shirt, I decide to wear nothing underneath as I use his soap to take a shower. I use the fluffy white towels and place his shirt over my naked body, and fold my clothes neatly with the towel. I open the door to an already changed Nate, in sweats, and no shirt. I place the clothes on a nearby chair in his room by the dresser. He looks at me in his white shirt and I walk up to him. He pulls me close against his body while he runs his hands through my hair and leans down to kiss my lips.

The kiss is slow, and he slides his tongue in, deepening the kiss. He lifts me up and my legs wrap around his waist, as he takes me to the bed, laying me on his pillow. He raises the shirt up over my head and kisses my stomach, slowly igniting my body as I run my fingers through his light brown hair. I moan as he takes my nipple into his mouth. He sucks one and then the other, sucking and twirling his tongue as I clench my thighs. He runs his tongue down my stomach to the area between my legs, while placing soft kisses on my skin.

He opens my legs further, swirling his tongue on my clit, and my pussy aches. I close my eyes, wanting to experience sex with someone who makes me feel alive, tired of wondering what it feels like to be touched by a man. He takes the lead, obviously knowing what he's doing, because I have no experience. I decide not to stop and give in to what we both want. I embrace the idea that if I find someone, I can please him just as much.

When his tongue laps my pussy, I tighten my fingers slightly through his hair, wanting more. "I want more. Don't stop, please," I plead.

He smiles against my pussy and sucks my clit, swirling his

tongue while he slides his finger inside me. "Fuck, you taste so good, baby," he says. My orgasm builds and I think I'm going to come all over his face as he continues to suck, increasing the pressure as I moan louder. "Come for me baby, I want to taste all of you." I close my eyes as he takes me over the edge. I come, my head tilting back, my pussy flooding in his mouth. He doesn't stop licking my pussy until it's clean of all my juices, swirling his tongue like he can't get enough.

He raises his head to look at me after the most intense orgasm I have ever had. "Your pussy is delicious, it tastes so sweet," he says softly, licking his lips, and it's the sexiest thing I have ever seen. I bite my lower lip as he lowers his sweatpants and raises himself gently over my body, holding just above me, trying to avoid crushing me with his weight. He looks down at my face, kisses me, and I can taste myself in his mouth, finding it so sexy. I break the kiss when I feel the tip of his hard cock at my entrance, my legs open to accommodate him, he pushes a little, and I wince in pain. I have read that it can hurt or feel uncomfortable the first time, I just didn't think that it would burn, but his cock is big and thick. I look at him as he frowns at me when my body tenses.

"Are you okay? Am I hurting you?" he asks. I look at him, my chest rising and falling, and it dawns on him. "You've never..." I shake my head, answering his question. "Shit. Are you sure you want me to..."

"Please don't stop."

"Okay. I will go slow, but if you tell me to stop, I will."

"Okay." I breathe in deep as he pushes little by little. He swallows and his eyes close, controlling the pace. I feel his cock stretching me inch by inch as he fills me entirely. He opens his eyes to look at my face, leaning in to kiss me as he moves. My hands run down his back toward his ass, pushing him deeper inside me, holding in the slight pain. He moves faster in and out and the pain eases, replaced by intense pleasure that has me breathing faster, and moaning.

"You're so tight, Giselle. You feel so fucking good, baby. I want to come inside you and make you mine. Only mine," he says as he kisses and sucks my neck.

"Faster, Nate. I'm going to come again." He pumps into me harder and harder, and my orgasm comes like a wave crashing and I scream his name, holding him. He grunts one last time and his hot cum spills inside me, flooding my pussy and lighting my body on fire.

He stays inside me and looks at me, and we stare at each other. "You gave me something beautiful that can only be given once," he whispers. I kiss him one last time as he pulls out and grabs the white T-shirt so that he doesn't drip cum mixed with blood. I hear the bathtub run and he returns to the bed, picking me up to place me in the warm bath. He grabs a washcloth, and he gently washes my swollen pussy with gentle strokes. I see him concentrating and when he is satisfied, he dries me off, and places me back on the bed like I'm a delicate flower. It is the most intimate thing to have a man bathe you after sex.

He looks up at me. "Are you okay?" he asks.

"Yes."

He lays with me on the bed and watches me go to sleep. I fall asleep in his arms, feeling warm as he holds me to his chest with my hair sprawled out.

The next morning, I squint when I feel the rays of the sun streaming through the french doors. I look over and see Nate sleeping soundly. When I move my head on his chest, he suddenly opens his eyes, and he bolts up from the bed, looking out through the french doors and realizes it's morning. He runs his hands through his hair.

"Are you okay, Nate?" I ask.

"I fell asleep," he says, confused.

"Yeah, we both did."

He looks at the time and I frown at what could be wrong. He lies back on the bed under the covers with me and holds me close. I climb on top of him, straddling him, and I feel his cock hardening under me. Rubbing my swollen pussy over it, I get wet as he runs his hands over my breasts down toward my waist. I place my hands on his chest and lift myself so my pussy can slide down his cock inch by inch, stretching me again. I close my eyes, enjoying the pleasure his cock gives me as I move my hips, riding his dick. He grabs my hips, and he sinks in deeper. I open my eyes and see desire in his eyes as he looks at my body riding him over and over.

His breathing picks up and his hands tighten on my hips, holding me there while I moan his name on my lips. He pumps into me while I ride him, milking his cock inside my wet pussy.

"This is mine. Don't you ever forget that this pussy belongs to me," he says. "You belong to me, Giselle. Say it."

I can't think while I'm riding his cock, as we are both about to come at the same time. I suck in my breath as the wave of my orgasm comes crashing and I raise my hands, sliding them into my hair. "I'm yours, Nate!" I scream while both of us come, filling each other. He sits up, kissing my chest, holding me. I open my eyes, lowering them to look into his, as my hands cup his face. We stay there looking at each other and something passes between us, but his eyes hold something powerful and possessive.

"We'd better get going," he says.

I dress in what I wore yesterday to meet Brie and Jaden in the kitchen. Brie and I are both wearing a tank top, a sweater with sneakers, and leggings. The kitchen island has an assortment of berries and fruits for breakfast. There is yogurt, juice, and even granolas over by the counter near the blender. I can see Nate making a specific shake with different powders and vitamins. I look over to Brie and she winks knowingly as I stare at Nate, watching his movements.

"We are going to take you girls shopping for the charity event tonight for kids who are disadvantaged. Nate and I donate every year, as his gym is part of the program. He offers to teach kids who want to learn how to defend themselves," Jaden says.

"It's amazing that you guys do that for kids," I say.

Brie looks over at Jaden and smiles. "We are honored you invited us, and you really don't have to take us shopping. If you could just take us..."

The blender starts, cutting off what I was about to say, and I look at Nate as he raises a brow. When the noise of the blender stops, he lifts the cup to drink. I eat the fruit with yogurt while Brie and I look over, waiting for him to speak.

"We are taking you girls shopping. I have already called Michelle to meet us at the store. She is a stylist and is well-known to help with these types of events. Please, it's all planned," Nate says.

Brie and I shrug our shoulders at the same time. "Okay," we both say, not wanting to argue, knowing they have made up their minds.

We finish eating breakfast and leave in two separate black Range Rovers that arrived to pick us up to take us to shop at all the designer boutiques. We meet a lady in her mid-forties with red hair. She ushers a giggling Brie to one dressing room and me to another, that is the size of our apartments back home. I'm alone with Michelle, and she eyes me, measuring my waist and bust size.

"Honey, you have a wonderful figure. No wonder you have Nate's attention, and your eyes are striking," she says.

I blush at her compliment. "Oh, thank you, but we are just friends. We're not..."

She waves her hand, dismissing what I was going to say. "Honey, that man has told me to dress you in everything Chanel. I think when a man is willing to pay almost one hundred grand to buy you clothes, I think you're past friends."

My eyes widen, like she has lost her mind. "Please don't let him spend that kind of money. It's really unnecessary."

She smiles. "Don't you worry about a thing. Relax and trust me, you will look perfect together." I stay quiet and wonder if Brie is feeling the same way. She put me in another room that is private with a door and gives me black lingerie to try on that is like satin bands being wrapped on my body, barely covering my nipples with a high-waisted thong all interconnected together. The only lace are two small triangle pieces over my nipples that can be clearly seen through the fabric.

Turning to look in the mirror, I don't recognize myself as the classy lingerie is clearly expensive, and something I could never afford. I turn to look at myself from the back and suddenly the door bursts open and in walks Nate, closing the door. I shriek and place my hands to cover myself, shocked at the intrusion, when he backs me against the wall, looking at my body slowly, admiring what he sees.

He grins, looking from my feet in Chanel heels, and up my body wrapped in lingerie. "What are you doing in here?" I ask. He slowly removes my hands covering my body and they fall to my sides. Then he grabs my throat slightly with no pressure, just one hand on my throat, and the other trailing his fingers outlining the lingerie on every part of my body slowly. I close my eyes as the sensation causes my thighs to squeeze together.

"I came to check up on what's mine. I couldn't wait another second knowing you're back here putting this on," he whispers.

A knock sounds on the door. "Nate, are you in there? She needs to try on the white and pink?" Michelle says through the door. He smiles, looking down at my wide eyes. He leans down to kiss me while he slides his finger into the folds of my pussy.

"Fuck, you're drenched. I'm dying to taste you on my lips again." My eyes dilate as I can smell his scent mixed with mint and cologne.

I bite my lower lip, wanting him, as I take in his black shirt that stretches over his wide chest with his beautiful eyes that match his gorgeous face. He kisses me on my cheek, removing his finger and sucking it into his mouth before he turns and opens the door. Michelle is waiting on the other side, not surprised that he is inside with me.

"Take them all. The pink, black, red, white, and make sure she wears one tonight," he tells her. She stands there with her mouth wide open as he walks around her, leaving me in the room staring at him, as he walks out.

She walks up and she smiles. "Just friends, huh?" she says sarcastically. I roll my eyes and giggle. She brings me the latest dress from the designer that is short, paired with fishnet stockings, the waist of the dress showing a glimpse of my stomach in cut outs. It's the most expensive dress I have ever worn.

I feel like a fairy princess as the day goes on with makeup, designer bags, and everything a girl could dream of. "Where is Brie?" I ask Michelle a while later.

"Getting the same treatment," she smiles.

With all the shopping completed, I finally get to see Brie alone at a café nearby outside the storefront. We look at each other, grinning. The cafe is French with crepes and Eiffel towers to complete the décor, and smelling like a French bakery once we're seated at the corner table. She looks at me with a smirk.

"You slept with him, didn't you?" Brie asks with a knowing smile.

"So? You slept with Jaden. I can tell you have that thoroughly fucked look on your face I have seen before."

"Yeah, but it's nothing compared to you. It was your first time, and you gave him your V-card."

I roll my eyes, tilting my head back. "I know, Brie. I just feel different when I'm around him and when he touches me, he lights me on fire, and he's the only one that can put it out."

"You have fallen for him, haven't you?" she asks.

I sigh.

I look at her thinking about how I feel. "I don't know, Brie. I'm scared, and I honestly don't know how I feel about him right now. He lives in a different world than we do and I don't see how it can work. I wanted my first time to be with someone I'm strongly attracted to where I can feel safe, and wanted. He is all of that and I have never felt what I feel with Nate."

"I get it, I don't blame you."

"So how about you and Jaden?"

She smiles and giggles. "Let's see. He's amazing, nice, funny, and he eats pussy like a porn star. I hope you couldn't hear my moans last night."

"You mean *our* moans," I say, as we laugh hysterically.

We finish at the café and head back to Nate's house to get ready for the evening charity event they invited us to. Brie and I decide to get ready in the guest room that I used when Nate requested me to come over and dance for him privately. I'm wearing the latest Chanel dress and the lingerie Nate wanted in the dressing room. I told Brie what happened earlier, and she giggled.

"He knows what he wants, apparently," she says.

"I guess. He is intense, and this is all knew to me. You know how my parents were when I was growing up."

I remember and wish they were still here, and my heart aches as the sadness briefly washes over me.

"Hey, they were the best parents a girl could ask for and you were lucky to have them as long as you did, even though they were taken from you too soon. It's better than being the daughter of the town whore."

I can't believe I'm so selfish and didn't stop to think of Brie's situation growing up with a drug addicted mom who turns tricks and an absent father. Look at what happened with Jace and his treatment of her when he didn't want to be seen with Brie because of who her mother was.

"I'm so sorry, Brie. I didn't stop to ask. How is your mother?"

She scoffs. "The same as always, asking for money and living in the trailer."

My eyes grow sad. "She still gets high on that stuff, doesn't she?"

"Yeah, I go to visit her once a week and sometimes there's an eviction notice. I have to pay to keep them from kicking her out, or having the electricity shut off."

The sadness in her eyes tells me the sorrow and anger she must feel. I know I would be disappointed and helpless to be the only one to deal with a mom like that. To know that she doesn't want help because she feels it's a daughter's duty to help their only parent.

"If you need anything, or money I can help you with, just let me know, and I will help you, Brie. You're the only person I have left," I tell her with tears in my eyes.

She is the only person in my life right now who I can count on to be there for me, and I would do anything to help my best friend. I have no family left, my parents have no other relatives, and I'm an only child with a lost dream. She gives me a big hug.

"We need to stop crying if we're to look good tonight, you know," she says, smiling with tears in her eyes.

Blinking back the tears in my eyes holding her in my arms, I whisper, "I love you, Brie."

"I love you, too. You're my sister, not just a best friend. Let's get ready and have a great time and learn to live life."

When finishing the last touches of our makeup, there is a knock on the door, and when I open it, I stay stunned, looking at a handsome Nate in a tuxedo. He absolutely takes my breath away. If I thought he looked good before, he looks even more gorgeous with his clean-shaven face and the intoxicating scent of his cologne. The tuxedo tailored to his frame, fitting like a glove. We stand there, gazing at each other, and I suddenly hear a clearing of a throat. I turn around to a smiling Brie.

"Are you two going to just stare at each other all night or are we going to a charity event?" she says.

My face flushes red and he smiles, looking at Brie. "I know, but your best friend looks beautiful, and I can't stop staring." He gives me his elbow and I immediately place my hand through it. We walk toward the foyer where Jaden awaits us. He smiles at Brie behind me, and he kisses her lightly on the lips.

"You look amazing and beautiful, both of you," Jaden says.

"So do you guys," I say. Turning to look at Nate, I say, "You look nice in a tux. I'm impressed."

"I'm glad you approve, gorgeous. Now let's go before it gets late."

* * *

When we arrive at the charity event, I am not prepared for the paparazzi and the flashing of lights on a red carpet. Looking at Brie, she eyes me nervously, feeling the same way. In my mind, I forgot who Nate is and the success he's had as a fighter. I read up on him and they consider him a ladies' man. I need to remind myself of that before I get too attached. I need to play this cool and not expect anything serious. He says I am his, but in the heat of passion, I know deep down that doesn't really mean I'm actually his. He actually paid me for a private dance with an NDA I needed to sign before he even let me in his house. The door of the black Escalade opens, and Jaden and Brie go out first to the first flash of cameras. Jaden is also popular as the amazing duo in MMA, as he is the most sought-after manager of an undefeated fighter.

When it's our turn, I can feel my stomach flutter in nervousness. He takes my hand and leads me out to the throng of people flashing their cameras calling out Nate's name, wondering who is the mystery girl he has brought to the charity event.

"What is she wearing?" one reporter asks. He answers her but gives no other information about what my name is or how we met. One even asked if he was off the market. He responds with "no comment," and we walk inside to a beautiful hotel on the Vegas strip. The ballroom is breathtaking, with many people in their gowns and tuxedos all laughing and drinking. We arrive at a specified table where Brie and Jaden are seated.

I look at Brie from across the table, who continues to look nervous in silence. Smiling back from across the table, I scan the crowd to look for Nate, and I find him talking to others, asking him about the donations to underprivileged children.

His gym offers a program to kids, a place to learn fitness, and self-defense. I listen intently and admire him for making a difference in the community, especially children who have no family. I have no family as an adult, having lost my parents, and can only imagine being abused and then placed in foster care. Brie grew up like that but managed not to be taken away and placed in foster care.

My parents always welcomed her to stay at the house. We were always together when I wasn't in dance or ballet, we would hang out after school every day until I left for Julliard, and we still stayed in touch.

Nate returns to the table and I give him a smile, finding him even more attractive than before. One of the older ladies at the table, who also donates to the charity and is a founder and real estate mogul from what I have overheard, eyes me curiously.

"So how did you meet Nate?" she asks.

I look up with a smile. "We met when he was visiting Sioux Falls," I say.

"Oh, wow. That is interesting. And what do you do, dear?"

Everyone at the table is nosey and wants to hear about the mystery girl Nate has brought to the event.

"I'm a dancer," I say. Brie looks at me with wide eyes.

"Oh, what kind of dance?" the woman asks. I will not tell her exactly what kind of dance, but some people are smirking and I can only imagine they can think I'm a glorified stripper.

"Ballet mostly," I say. You can see the look of confusion on everyone's face.

"Really?" she asks, shocked. "Well, come to think of it, you have the figure. Where did you go to school?" I try to hold in my annoyance at her twenty questions. I'm definitely not revealing any exact truths here and decide vague answers are best. Nate is quiet and is about to interject when I place a hand on his arm to stop him.

"Upstate, I studied dance and ballet, nowhere exciting," I say.

"I see," she says, ending the conversation.

Thank God the rest of the evening goes smoothly.

Nate looks at me. "Are you okay?" he asks.

I assure him. "Yes, of course. I'm fine." He doesn't look convinced, but doesn't pry further. Never have I felt more uncomfortable in my life and I realize Nate and I have never really talked much about each other.

I would like to get to know him better on a personal level, not just sex and going out to charity events. I know being in the public eye is a challenge, but I'm interested in him, and not being in the constant eye of the public. Most women he's used to are superficial that way, from what I have read, but my parents did not bring me up to be like that.

I look over to Brie. She must feel the same, an outcast. We work in a diner and dance at a club. We eye each other in silent communication that we cannot wait to leave. All these people, looking, judging, trying to find a flaw they can make a big deal out of. When you look at Nate and Jaden, they don't even have a clue how Brie and I are feeling. They are smiling and talking to other people, and we are just sitting there like arm candy, and it's then that I realize they brought us here for show, and nothing more. When introductions are made it's, "This is Brie or Giselle," not even, 'my good friend' before our names. *Just another girl I brought along*. They could have saved the money and just let us wear whatever and introduced us as Coco and Money Monroe, would have saved them the trouble.

Brie and I stay quiet the rest of the night, only smiling and speaking when needed to fake farewells and goodbyes. The guys don't say a word on the way back to Nate's house and there is a slight tension in the air. Jaden takes Brie to the guest room and I follow Nate to his bedroom. He turns, shuts the door, and looks at me with desire. He slides my dress off my arms and unzips the side, revealing the lingerie. I squeeze my thighs from the heat pooling there as he looks me up and down. I bite my bottom lip as I can't help the way I feel when he looks at me or when he touches my skin; I feel heat that floods my core like liquid lava. He takes off his jacket and unbuttons his shirt, revealing his smooth, muscular chest. He removes his belt and stands clad in his socks and boxer briefs. I walk him back so he can sit on the bed while I kneel in front of him between his legs.

I have never given a man a blow job before, but Brie took me to the back room at the club where I watched Treasure and Diamond give blow jobs to very special clients. I learned how to relax your throat muscles to take a man's cock all the way down without gagging.

I've never tried it firsthand, and I wanted to give Nate that pleasure. He looks at me kneeling in front of him and he rubs his thumb over my bottom lip. I stick my tongue out to stroke his thumb and he sucks in a breath as he runs his fingers through my hair. Sliding his boxers down, releasing his massive erect cock, thick, and ready to be sucked.

Suddenly I notice the scars of what look like burn marks, angry red marks all over his inner thighs. I frown and take a deep breath at the angry marks I know do not come from fighting. I slide my fingers one and caress it. He grips my hand tight, stopping me from touching him.

"What happened?" I ask as I look up into his eyes.

What I find there is anger, cold and hard. "Nothing," he snaps. He gets up, making me fall back on my heels. Watching him as he stands, I realize I couldn't have noticed before because of the position we were in yesterday. "Nate, I'm sorry… I shouldn't, I…"

I stop as he looks down at me with a coldness I don't recognize. I feel like I did something wrong, but I really just wanted to know what happened to him so I can understand him. I didn't think he would get this angry.

"I think it's best if you sleep in the guest room tonight. You will go back early tomorrow," he says. I'm still sitting on the carpeted floor in front of the bed as he walks toward the bathroom speaking to me in a cold, hard tone. It's like he can't stand the sight of me and wants me gone.

"Nate, look, I'm sorry. If I did…"

He interrupts me again. "Are you on the pill? You know, to make sure you don't…" I frown at his change of subject. I don't let him continue.

I honestly hadn't even thought of that and I can't believe I'm so stupid and didn't think about contraception or falling pregnant. It's like a bucket of ice-cold water on my face and I suddenly get angry with mostly myself for letting a man who clearly sees me as a piece of ass from a dance club have sex with me unprotected. Of course, he expected me to be on the pill.

"Of course, I will make sure. I'll take care of it," I say coldly. I get up from the floor, giving him my back, not letting him see the hurt of his words and the pain he is inflicting.

I pick up the dress from the floor, slip into it so I can walk back shamefully to the guest bedroom, not forgetting the way he made me feel tonight. Once my hand is on the door handle to open it, he speaks and I stop.

"I just want to make sure since I was careless last night and did not use protection, I'm clean and get tested regularly."

What an asshole. Tears suddenly fill my eyes and I don't turn around, but swallow the enormous ball in my throat as I stiffen. "Of course," I whisper, I hurriedly walk out of his room, not looking back, wishing I could be anywhere but here.

Once inside the guest bedroom, I strip from the clothes he bought me and neatly place everything in the garment bags. I quickly change back into the clothes that I came in with, lying on the bed, letting the tears I have been holding in fall, as I hold in the sobs that won't stop. If this is what heartbreak feels like, I prefer to be dead than to feel the emptiness my soul feels right now at being alone with no one to hold me, or to love me.

Nate will not let me in and just wants me on his terms and when I get close, he shut me out. He obviously doesn't want me in his life that way. I am no better than any woman he sleeps with. What I thought was special, or maybe some type of understanding, was just a lie. I, being the naïve virgin, fell for the charms of a man who sleeps with women and has a goodie bag for them after coming through.

I saw the signs. Brie was right in telling me to be careful because she knew I would feel for him. I realize he is dark inside, living alone with no one, broken, and can't be mended. Getting my overnight bag ready, I decide I don't want to take anything he has bought for me. I realize I have to ask Brie to take me to the clinic back home so I can get a morning after pill and birth control along with some tests. I will forward him proof of everything so he doesn't wonder and contact me about it. I can't blame him, I was careless myself.

I text Brie and tell her I want to leave and give her a short rundown of what happened. She says she will wait until Jaden falls asleep, since she had an awkward night after the event. We decide to order an Uber to wait for us on the road leading to Nate's house based on the map of our location. I meet her at the door leading to a small, modern sitting area with a french door that leads to the driveway of the house. There is a walkway we can go through that leads to the entrance. We hold hands and walk up the road with only the possessions we came with. Brie and I think alike, not needing flashy dresses or purses to make us feel whole. The Uber is there to take us to the nearest major airport. We purchase the next flight to Sioux Falls, and thank God we can book it while I tell her everything.

"What an ass. I can't believe he treated you like that after you just wanted to know."

"I know. I should have listened to you when you told me to be careful. Lesson learned. I don't want to see or hear from him again. Can you please take me to the clinic? I'm going to send him the papers with the clinic's information and results."

"Of course. Giselle, please don't cry."

Sniffing, I try to smile. "It's because I thought... I don't know what I thought. I'm just a stupid girl, what did I expect?"

She looks at me with sadness and pain. "Yeah, Jaden was acting weird since we left the event, and I didn't know how to tell him I was uncomfortable. It was like we were there to just be there and look pretty like an object that isn't good enough to speak. It was awful. I was so relieved when you called me, but sad at the same time because I knew something was wrong."

"Let's go back to our side of the tracks. There is no room for girls like us in their world."

10
NATE

What the fuck did I just do? I just kicked her out of my room and treated her no better than a paid whore. Fuck!

I run my fingers through my hair. I wasn't ready to see the pity in her eyes when she saw the burns my father inflicted on me when I was a kid. It was how he would wake me up to get to school. The pain I would feel every morning, a reminder when she rubbed her soft fingers up my thighs, the pleasure shadowed over the memory of the pain. The marks were a cruel, sick tactic my father would use after my mother died. I couldn't even get back at him for the years of abuse he put my mother and I through. My mom would just be in another universe when he inflicted the pain every day. When he was drunk, it would get worse.

The look in her eyes when she looked up at me caused me pain, and I'm ashamed at treating the most beautiful girl I have touched and lay my eyes on like shit.

To see the pity in her eyes when she found out my father abused me as a child, neglected by a heroin addicted mother, made fun of at school and bullied because my parents were broke junkies. No one knows except Jaden.

We were both raised in the foster system as teenagers with careless attitudes, destined to be dead or in jail. I couldn't tell her, open up to her, or let her sleep with me in the same bed. I didn't want her to see me wake up, screaming from the nightmares. It scared me when I fell asleep after we had sex. What if I attacked her or hurt her from one of my nightmares? I would die before I hurt her physically. The demons that come for me at night will not spare her, they will consume her, letting her see the darkness that exists inside me. It's a part of me that no one sees, a part of me I feed in the cage so I can function. Fighting is my life, and it's all I have to keep me from being consumed by the complete darkness that awaits me every night.

When she told me she never had sex and that she was a virgin with just a nod, I was shocked. Never did I think in my wildest dreams that a girl as beautiful as she hadn't been touched. I was sure that football jerk, Bresely, had fucked her. Thinking about it, it's the fact that he hasn't that has him sniffing like a lost puppy. The way she dances, so beautiful and sexy, because Giselle Monroe is a talented dancer and choreographer. I overheard her parents died in a car accident and she had to sell everything to settle their debts. It's probably why she dances with Brie. Jaden really likes Brie, but he is guarded, just as I am, not letting anyone in.

In the middle of the night at 3:29 a.m., I wake up in cold sweats, thinking my father is burning my thighs, covering my mouth so I can't breathe, trying to wake me up and gasping for air. I place my hands over my sweaty face. I take a shower, thinking about how I'm going to face Giselle after I treated her. I quickly get dressed and walk toward the kitchen to see Jaden sitting alone with his hands over his face, nursing a cup of coffee.

He senses my presence and lowers his hands, and I see a solemn look on his face. "What's up?" I ask.

"They're gone."

I frown, taken aback. "What do you mean, gone? We have to take them back."

He shakes his head. "They left last night after we fell sleep. They left, Nate. I was a total asshole to her, and I would have done the same."

I quickly head to the guest bedroom. Sure enough, it's empty except for everything I bought for her. She left everything neatly in its package as if no one had touched it. I can still smell her sweet scent in the room and I take my phone from my pocket. I decide to call her to at least see if she made it back okay. I am walking back to the kitchen where I left Jaden. He looks up.

"I tried, she will not answer you," he says.

I try texting her and it's marked as delivered but unread. "Fuck!" I close my eyes.

"Look, we have a fight to prepare for and we need to concentrate on the plan. You need to train, and hard. There is another fight after this one and we can't fuck around. It will give things time to cool down."

I sit on the stool on the island and give it some thought. "Maybe you're right. I can't get caught up right now. I need to train. I have the gym and the program for the kids. We will catch up with them when things cool off. Give her some time." Trying to sound convincing, we both know that it's going to take a little more than that, but I am not ready to open myself up and explain. We don't even know each other that well, just on an intimate level.

One thing I know about Giselle is that she tastes like heaven. I have to concentrate on my next fight and the one after. I have never not used a condom, and she is the first where I didn't think about using one. She was so soft and tight, her pussy wet,

I lost my mind needing to come inside her, claiming her, making her mine.

I couldn't stop thinking about how tight her pussy was, milking my cock in the morning, that I couldn't wait to see her in the lingerie at the store. I wanted to buy all the lingerie in the entire store just to see her in it, with her perfect tits and ass. I knew when I slid my finger into her folds she would be soaked and ready for me. Almost taking her right there, not caring if everyone heard her cries when I filled her, making her come.

The event went well except for the questions everyone was asking about her. Who was she? Where did we meet? She answered better than I could have imagined, and they tempted me to tell them she was my girlfriend, but I knew it would be wrong to lie and didn't know how she would feel. I could see myself with someone like her, genuine, and caring.

I hurt her, and maybe it's for the best she isn't with someone like me. She is better off with someone who doesn't hide from her or keep her at a distance. I decide to tell Jaden that it's best to leave it alone. I turn on the TV and see the entertainment news. Of course, there is a report of me with her and a picture of us at the event with Jaden and Brie in the background. The reporter is wondering if I'm in a relationship with a mystery girl no one knows. That she is beautiful and must be a model clad in head-to-toe Chanel. She really looks beautiful in that dress on my arm. All night I had to stomach men looking at her beautiful, toned legs with hungry lust in their eyes. I almost punched one asshole ogling her while she sat at the table and was adjusting herself. When I gave him a hard stare, he nervously looked away, knowing I was going to punch him the fuck out for looking at my girl.

I keep telling myself she isn't my girl. She must think I don't want her, and with the way I treated her, I couldn't blame her if she never wanted to see my face again. I'm so fucked with my emotions all over the place...

I get a text later after my workout in my home gym after Jaden left to his house. I get anxiety when I see it's from her, my heart pounding heavily in my chest when I open the attachment that was sent.

My insides turn cold, making me feel like a total piece of shit. In my face is a doctor's test result that shows Giselle Monroe with all her information from a town clinic, negative test results from every STD test you can take.

My stomach sinks as I scroll to the next page and see she took a morning after pill and the medications they gave her to kill any possibility that she could have fallen pregnant with my baby. I close my eyes, hating myself for what I did to her, the words I can't take back, the hurt I have caused her, crushing the most beautiful moment she gave me.

I unleash my fury on the punching bag until my knuckles are raw and bleeding and it still isn't enough.

The following night, I can't sleep. The nightmares are worse than they have ever been. This time a voice says they are going to get her and make her pay. I wake up swinging like a fucking psycho, screaming.

11

GISELLE

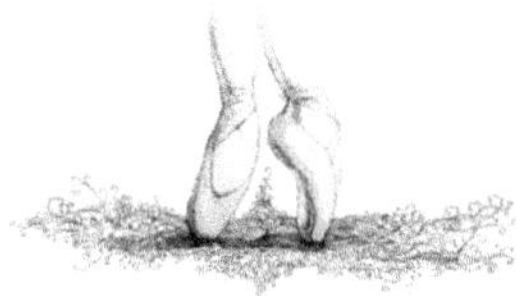

I sent the text with the proof he requested. He can see that I was never on the pill, but so what? I took every precaution to make sure I wouldn't fall pregnant with a baby he wouldn't want, covering every base I could at the clinic. I needed to make up the money, since the flight and clinic set me back from my goal. I figure I can save enough to open a dance studio to teach kids to dance and perform ballet. It's what I love and what I'm good at. I receive a call from the girls at Juilliard who told me to come to New York and they can get me in the dance company, but I can't leave Brie here on her own. New York is a big place, and it's expensive to live. Dean wants to visit, to see where I am dancing, not judging, but has heard of it through social media. He wants to record one of my dances and never got around to send me my last piece before my parents died. During everything, I totally forgot about it. I worked hard on that piece, but it earned me enough to graduate. I can't wait to see what Dean did with it. He wanted to be a composer but is very good with editing.

Brie and I never made it to the football game we had tickets for, and I mention it to her in case Jason came by the club. I told him we would go, but were caught up with Nate and Jaden and totally forgot.

It is Tuesday and the beginning of fall in the air, with cooler temperatures that are nice when taking a walk outside. Brie and I are working at the diner when Jason and Jace come in and sit at a booth. I walk up to them to take their order, hoping the encounter goes smoothly. "What can I get you boys?" Jason looks at me with his soft green eyes and it reminds me of a long time ago when we are under that tree. I get the same vibe from him that doesn't make me melt, and sense it's more than friendly.

"I would like you to honor your promise to me and go see me play." Looking at him, I really shouldn't have accepted the invitation.

I'm about to turn him down when Brie walks up looking from the TV and says, "She accepts." I look at her like she has lost her mind, when from the corner of my eye, I see Nate from his recent fight in all his glory grabbing a marker from a blonde with her breasts spilling out from her bra, while he circles her waist and she whispers in his ear, he signs his name giving her a personal autograph over her left breast. The hurt I feel is gut wrenching and my throat constricts to see it on national television. It's plain as day. Almost a month has gone by, and he is obviously back to his old self.

He hasn't called me since I sent him the results from the clinic or come to see me at the club. I didn't expect to hear from him and I understand when someone doesn't want me. I am lost in my thoughts when I look at Jason, who is waiting for me to respond.

"Okay, I will honor my word and go to one of your games."

His eyes light up. "Really? Are you sure, Giselle? If you really don't want to, I understand," he says. Jason is a really handsome guy, he just isn't Nate. Nate is a bad boy with a face like a model and the body of a god. He also treated me worse than a fifty-dollar high school bet on a kiss from a girl.

"I will go, but as friends"

He swallows, and he looks at me. "I was always your friend, Giselle. I just made a stupid high school mistake in taking money for something I always wanted." I blush, not expecting him to say it aloud.

Jace smirks. "Yeah, Brie, we did things that were stupid but committed acts that we always wanted. You were my girl first."

He stays looking at her with desire and I know he is referring to the time when Brie gave him her V card.

I clear my throat. "The usual for you boys, the traditional breakfast with orange juice?" I ask. They both nod.

"We will pick you girls up on Friday for the game," Jason says.

"Okay, we will be ready at 5 p.m. at our place."

"We know where it is," Jace says. I'm not surprised they know where we live. In a small town, word travels fast. When they're finished, they give us a big tip, like last time. Jason grabs my hand before I turn to go. I look at his hand on mine and he releases his hold. If it was Nate, I would have gotten flushed and wet with goosebumps. I kick myself inside my thoughts, always thinking about him. I need to remind myself that he doesn't want me.

"Are you seeing anyone?" he asks.

"You mean if I'm seeing Nate 'The Reaper' Phoenix?" He nods. I look at the television, replaying the entertainment channel where Nate signs the girl's breast. He follows my gaze, and he watches the same thing. I turn to look back at him. "That should answer your question."

I clear the table as he gets up to leave in his white, fitted T-shirt and blue jeans. It's a shame I don't feel the instant pull, but attractive he most definitely is. He stops before he leaves and says, "He doesn't deserve someone as beautiful as you. See you Friday." When he passes by me, I can smell his cologne that I will soon compare to the man who caused me many sleepless nights.

Brie walks up to me and says, "I'm sorry I accepted for you like that, I just saw the TV, and it pissed me off for you."

"It's okay, I get it, you're tired of me moping around."

"He really likes you, and I think he always has. It will be great for you to go out and get a change of pace."

"How about you and Jaden?"

"It was just sex. He doesn't want me. Imagine when he finds out where I come from, or finds out who my mom is," she says.

"Yeah, I guess you're right. We need to go out with friends and have fun. We are young and single."

Friday comes quicker than expected. Brie is at my apartment, and we are drinking some white wine, wearing jean shorts and tank tops with a raven logo to support the team. I can hear a loud muffle of a truck pull up since I'm on the lower apartment floor. I hear a knock on the door and it's Jason and Jace wearing wind breakers that are part of their team uniform to pick us up. They smile and hand us special passes with lanyards around our necks. I catch Jason looking at my ass when I turn around to leave my apartment. He turns red and runs his hand over his face. "I'm sorry, Giselle. Didn't mean to..."

I hold up a hand. "I get it, you're a guy. Just make sure I don't catch you all the time."

I don't mean to flirt, but it must be the wine.

We walk up to Jason's big, black, lifted truck with big tires. I'm glad it has electronic floorboards so I can get in without climbing to open the door. Once inside, the plush leather seats hug me as I sit in the front with Jason, while Brie and Jace sit in the back.

We reach the players' entrance of the football stadium. They are playing here in our home state even though they are the opposing team. We enter and Jason places his hand on my lower back, and I let him. He leads us to our seats close to the players below. Some players pass and recognize Brie and I from the club. They stop and smile, looking at Jason and Jace, the popular duo, and the stars of the team. The game starts and the Ravens have the lead just after halftime. Brie and I cheer when there is a key play that has Jason scoring, we rise and cheer him on as he runs with the football toward us with the camera following us on national television. He runs up the edge of the stand and gives me a kiss on the cheek and throws me a jersey with his name on it.

Jace throws the game ball at Brie and blows her a kiss, and the crowd goes wild cheering. We smile and the camera is on them while they dance on the field. The game is a win for the Ravens, with many highlights aired on TV. The energy is from the win, as we head out of the stand meeting face to face with Jason.

"I came to get you so we can go hang out after."

"Where?" I ask.

"We go with some players to this sports bar where there is dancing and music."

I look at Brie, and she clearly wants to go, so I decide to

agree. "Okay." He gets excited and carries me playfully on his back to his truck after his shower. He smells clean and all male as I hold on to him around his neck as he grips his hands on my thighs.

He places me in his truck, and we all head over to the sports bar he mentioned. When we arrive, most of the team is there with other professional athletes who play sports to celebrate the big win. Brie and I laugh as we take two shots, the last one almost goes down the wrong way and I cough, laughing with Brie. We dance to the beat of the music as the alcohol does its job, taking away the last month of grief and heartache. It wasn't like he was my boyfriend or anything, I tell myself we don't owe each other anything. So why does it hurt? I don't know about anything anymore, but I hate feeling this way. My life has just been about loss lately and grief of losing the ones you care about.

Brie and I are dancing and suddenly I feel a hand come up from behind me to circle my waist. Brie smiles behind me, letting me know it's someone familiar. I turn my head to the side and it's Jason, and I smile at his friendly embrace. He doesn't come up behind me too close, which I can appreciate. I sway to the music, having a great time as Jace dances next to Brie, having a good time, reminding me of old times when we would all hang out at my parent's farm. We dance for a while and need to take a break. Looking at Jason, I lean in toward his ear to tell him that Brie and I are going to get a drink of water. The alcohol has me feeling dizzy. He smiles and nods, releasing his light hold on me. We make it back to the bar and I order water. I look over at Brie and her eyes go wide, looking over my shoulder.

"What's wrong?" I ask as I turn my head to the left and freeze. Standing right next to me is Nate with a murderous look on his face. Brie stays silent, but Nate gets closer to me with the latest marks on his face from his last fight. I can see a cut on his lip and slight bruising on his right eye, looking like it hurts. His hands rest on the bar as he looks at me and he sneers in thought.

"Seems like you're having a good time," he says. I can still feel the pull of desire only he can make me feel. I wonder how he knew we were here tonight. I seethe in rage that after everything, I can't believe he feels entitled to talk to me this way in his sarcastic drawl.

Smiling and showing indifference, I decide to answer. "Actually, I'm having a great time." I turn to Brie, giving him my back as I sip my water. She looks nervous. "Let's go back," I tell her. When I go to leave the bar, he blocks my path and I look up at him. His eyes take me in, looking at my chest and down to my shorts. "What do you want, Nate?"

He sucks in a deep breath and rubs his hand through his hair. "Look, I want to talk."

"There is nothing to say. You have had plenty of time to reach out to me and you have obviously been busy with your little groupies. You were very clear about what you wanted when we last spoke and I did what you wanted. I took care of it, like a big girl." He steps closer, giving me no room to leave or breathe.

"Are you fucking him?"

My eyes go wide. "Really, Nate? Are you kidding me right now?"

"Tell me." He leans close to my ear and whispers, "Does he make your pussy wet like I do? Because if he has touched what's mine, I'm going to break his fucking face." I pull away even though my pussy is so wet with the scent of his cologne, the memory of him filling me, making me scream his name, while I come undone in his arms.

"Nate, you can't just come around and break his face because he likes me or touches me. It doesn't work that way."

I see Jason come up behind him. "Is everything okay, Giselle?" Jason interrupts. I smile at him.

"Yeah, Nate was just saying hi," I say.

Nate turns and looks at him in his face. "I was just seeing how my girl was doing," he sneers.

"Last time I checked, she wasn't your girl, and if the news is anything to go by, looks like you have your hands full after your last fight."

I can see Nate clenching his fist and I don't want Jason to get into anything because Nate will fight him. I step in between them. "Look, please don't do this right now." I know Nate can kill Jason if he goes after him, and I can't let that happen.

I calm down once I see them looking at me.

"Nate, Jason and are friends and we were all out having a good time. Please, just back off before we attract more attention."

"Then let me take you home," Nate says. I look at Jason and Nate, weighing my options.

I look at Jason, and he nods in understanding. "Are you sure, Giselle? I can take you home," Jason says.

"It's okay, Jason. I'll let him take me home. I wanted to at least tell you we had an amazing time," I say, with a soft smile. He smiles and I look at Brie, who is talking to Jaden. I didn't even notice they were ten feet away with a seething Jace looking over from his table.

"I will take her home," Nate says, standing next to me. I look over at him with a serious face.

"I'm leaving with you to give you the opportunity to talk and not cause trouble to someone who has been respectful and nice to me."

"Was this before or after he made it known on national television that he wants you?"

"I don't belong to you, Nate, you made sure of that, or did you forget?"

He pinches his nose and takes my hand to guide me out the sports bar.

We walk out to the parking lot and there is a black Bentley he unlocks with a key fob. He opens the door and I get in the passenger side.

"How did you know I was here?" I ask as he gets in the driver's side. The alcohol has made me a little courageous in speaking my mind.

He looks at me as he turns on the car. "I saw you on TV and lost my fucking mind when I saw him kissing you on the cheek, took the next flight out on my private plane, and my publicist got me this car when I landed." He drives out and takes me home. We reach my apartment, and he gets out of the car after he parks it in the space.

"What are you doing?" I ask.

He smiles. "I am going inside to see your apartment and talk."

"Why?"

"Because, I want to."

Taking in a deep breath, he follows me inside my apartment as he closes the door. He looks around and I feel vulnerable. He must hate my apartment compared to his house. It is small with minimal furniture and nothing he is used to. It just reminds me how different we truly are. He looks at some pictures of me and Brie and the two of my parents. He picks up the one of my parents embracing Brie and I.

"These are your parents?" he asks.

"Yeah," I sigh.

"You look like your mom but have your dad's hair. Must have been nice having parents who look at you like you're their everything."

"They are my everything. That picture shows the only family I have. Now it's just Brie," I say sadly.

"It's how I feel about Jaden. He is my best friend, manager, and I trust him completely. How did your parents pass, if you don't mind me asking?"

I look down as I sit on the edge of my bed. "They died in a car accident when I was away at school. I received a call that they were involved in an accident on the highway, and they didn't survive. I had to come back from school, and I almost didn't graduate. Luckily, I completed my senior piece and under the circumstances..." I sigh, "They passed me."

"That's because you're that good." I look up at him as he leans on the doorway to my bedroom.

"I'm not that good," I say. He pushes off the door and comes to stand in front of me, lifting my chin with his finger, and looks at me.

"Sweetheart, I have never seen someone so talented. I'm not even into dancing and I would pay to see you."

"Are you trying to get me to have sex with you?" I say laughingly, lightening the mood. He bursts out laughing and I can see his perfect white straight teeth with that smile that can melt any woman's panties clean off. He is that breathtaking, his body is carved in perfection, molded in all the right places.

He stops laughing and leans close to my ear. "Come home with me, please. I want you with me. I need to train for my next fight, and I want you with me," he whispers.

I look up at him. "What about work and Brie?"

"She can come on her days off and you can come for two days to work, but if you don't want to work, I'll pay for anything you need. I would like for you to help me with the kids at the gym. Some of them have little sisters and there is a dance studio on the corner."

My eyes light up when he mentions the dance studio. I would like to learn how to operate one. It's what I'm saving for and even Brie can help me run it. I don't think about it further and decide it's a great opportunity, but don't want to make the same mistake as last time. I think it's best we are friends, and if his intentions are really as they seem, then he shouldn't mind.

"Okay. But..."

"Name it. Anything."

"We go as friends, and no promises." He gets serious about my statement.

He stays silent for a bit, contemplating. "Alright, get ready. My plane leaves in an hour."

I clean up, and pack everything I might need. I call the club and will work only two days and one day a week at the diner. Brie will come on her days off and I will come with her the day Nate is training all day and will not see him. Brie calls me and lets me know that Jaden and Nate had already planned this and if I was okay with it. I tell her I have nothing to lose.

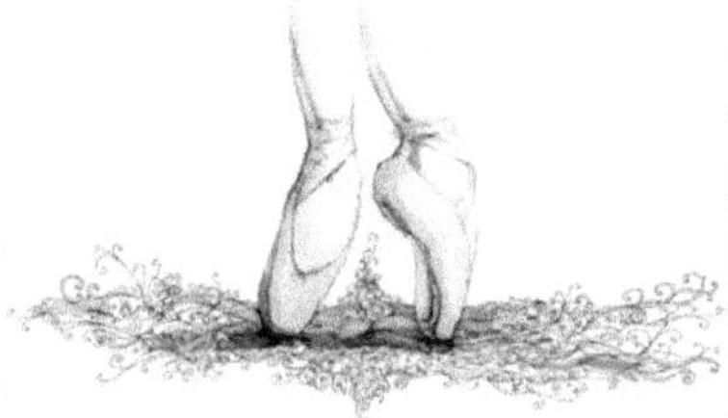

We land and I'm taken back to Nate's house. When we arrive, I head toward the guest bedroom. "Where are you going?" I point in the direction of the guest bedroom.

"Friends, remember?"

He shakes his head. "Nah, you're staying with me, beautiful. When I meant you were staying with me, you were staying with me in my house, my room, with me. Come on, I need to get to the gym in the morning. The kids have Saturday practice, and you can meet Lenora at the dance studio. I kind of let her know she was meeting you." He winks. He so sure of himself.

"What if I did not agree to come?"

"Then I guess I would have looked stupid," he says. I don't want a repeat of him and his changing moods, so I stand my ground and take the guest bedroom.

"I'm still going to stay in the guest room."

"If that's where you feel comfortable, then fine." I can tell he is little bothered by my decision, but If I plan on staying and not fall victim to his change of mood, then it's for the best.

He's a mystery living in this big white house alone, fighting and training. He won't open up to me and let me in, and I can't risk my feelings. I sense it's because he doesn't trust me enough.

"I will knock in the morning if I don't see you. We need to be at my gym at 8:30 in the morning."

"Okay. Good night."

"Good night, Giselle." He slowly walks toward his room. I would give anything to be in his bed and fall asleep in his arms, but the risk of feeling the sting of his rejection is still fresh like a wound that is trying to heal. My heart is fragile right now, and as much as I want any part of him, I can't risk feeling that pain.

Remembering his rejection and treatment the last time I was here, I need my guard up because as much as I want him, he has this power over me, a power that takes a part of me I can never get back, even if that part of me is lost.

I'm invisible. The only way I know I'm here is if I dance. Dance brought me here, not me. The real me he doesn't know. The real Nate, he will not let me find. The question is, why?

The morning light streams through the window of the bedroom, and I wake up and get ready before he knocks on the bedroom door. Once I get to the kitchen and find a light breakfast, I take a seat to wait for Nate. I'm eating a strawberry when he comes dressed in a matching hoodie and sweatpants. The hoodie has the Grim Reaper on it and I realize it fits his personality. I'm ready in a leotard under my black windbreakers, and my hair in a messy bun on top of my head. I slide off the stool, grab my small bag with my phone as I watch him with a serious expression, it's as if he had the worst night ever.

"Are you okay?"

"Yeah, let's go."

He sounds annoyed with me asking and doesn't even make eye contact. I am taken aback by his strange mood. I remember him telling me he is not a morning person, so I follow him at a distance with a protein shake in one hand, not saying a word. He grabs his keys to walk outside to his car. We reach the white supercar, and he stays silent, not looking at me. I decide to leave him be. I slide into the car and look out the window as he drives toward his gym. We stay silent until we reach the parking lot. I decide to ask, not knowing what I should do next.

"Um, do I—" We are out of his car and I follow him as stiffens, he turns toward me, making me stop mid-stride, almost running into him.

"The dance studio is over there and some of the younger sisters of the boys sit and watch the other kids that have parents pay for lessons." He points over to a dance studio in the corner building.

"Okay," I say as I squint over in the direction of the dance studio where I can see three little girls standing through the window to watch what is going on inside.

"I told Lenora about you, you can go, and I will be inside. I have training," he says curtly and walks inside the gym, leaving me standing outside alone.

What is his problem? I can't remember what I did wrong. One moment he wants me here with him and the next, my presence annoys him. He didn't even walk with me to introduce me or anything. It's like he wants me to disappear. I think I made a mistake in coming here with him, but I'm here and we are just friends. I walk up to open the door to see a class being given by an older woman with fifteen girls, ranging from seven to about thirteen. I see the three little girls watching with excitement and longing in their eyes, watching the other girls in their cute little ballerina outfits.

"Can I help you?" The older women comes over, eyeing me.

"Yes, Nate told me to come over. He said he mentioned me. Are you Lenora? My name is Giselle."

"Ah, yes. He mentioned you. He says you're a very talented dancer from Sioux Falls."

"I guess you could say that, but not really."

She continues to look me over. "Sweetheart, you're not just a dancer, I bet my dance studio. You're a ballerina, with your figure and tone."

My face flushes and she can see that she figured me out. "Let me see." She waves me inside to the main room where the young girls are listening to our conversation, waiting eagerly.

"I have a special request."

"What is that, dear?" She raises a thin arched brow.

"The three girls over there get lessons, and I'm willing to pay for them. How much is the rest of your season?" I ask. I know the feeling of wanting to dance at that age, and those are little girls who are probably in the foster care system.

"If it's okay with Nate. He would have to get signed permission for all three young girls, and it's twelve hundred each. There can only be one sibling in the program, so that is why they can't join," she says.

I look over at the three young angelic faces, one blonde about 5 years old, one brunette about 9 years old, and one about 10 years old. Their eyes light up, hoping they can get the same lessons as the other girls looking at me like I have lost my mind. I take out my debit card and know I will have to make up the money, but I don't care. I can't sit here and dance with this woman while three young girls who have nothing sit there and watch. I just can't.

"Here, charge your fee on my card," I say. She widens her eyes as she takes my card to ring me up.

"All three?" she asks.

Determined, I look at her in the eyes. "All three. And I will help you out, I don't want you to pay me. I will teach them the basics, so your other students don't fall behind."

"Alright, first show me what you know."

"Okay," I walk into the middle of the dance floor while the three girls say thank you and hug me with tears in their eyes. I smile and look over at Lenora. "Ready?"

I dance with my dance shoes and perform just like if I was at Julliard, and when I'm done, Lenora stands with her mouth open in awe. "Well, I see I was right after all. He doesn't know, does he?" she asks shaking her head.

"About what?" I ask with a straight face.

"That you're a ballerina. He thinks you're just some dancer. If he only knew you're a ballerina with many years of experience and training you can only get from one place I recognize." The girls are looking at us as we continue our conversation. She walks up to me. "I went there too, and I can see it. I see you, Giselle."

"I'm not that person anymore," I say sadly.

She breathes deep. "I don't know what happened to you, but I got hurt and couldn't continue. You are still young and have a chance. It will be an honor for you to come here and help with our new students. I will provide them with uniforms and slippers." I smile.

"Thank you, Madame." She smiles.

The youngest of the three, a blond little girl named Cindy, comes up to me in excitement. "You're a real ballewina," she says in her cute little voice. “I want to be a real one just like you.”

“Of course, you can be anything you want,” I say, as I kneel to get a better look at her. She gives me a big hug with her blue eyes and straight blonde hair. She is adorable.

“Thank you.” My eyes fill with tears I will not let fall. The other two girls give me hugs and thank me for the lessons with smiles and gratitude.

When the lessons are over, and I teach the new girls the basics, they are so happy and excited as they walk over to the gym. I follow them since I have never been there and don’t know where to go. We enter inside and see a desk with a man in his forties siting behind it. I look over and there is a group of teenage boys learning the basics of mixed martial arts. In the middle of the gym, in the cage, is where I see Nate sparring with another guy. There are other guys from his team outside the cage giving him instructions I can’t make out. They’re all big guys with tattoos. Nate suddenly takes his opponent down hard, ending in a lumbar where he taps out. Nate lets up and stands with the sweat dripping down his torso. Even sweaty, he looks good with his muscles on display to perfection. He takes his gloves off with his teeth and opens the cage door. He spots me and I look down at Cindy as she rushes at him.

“Nate! Nate!” she says. I suddenly hear Lenora say hello to the gentleman at the desk named Charles. I turn around and as she passes by me in the direction where Nate is kneeling, talking to Cindy. The other two girls follow behind Lenora.

“Nate, I need a word with you,” Lenora says. The other guys who were standing by the cage walk up behind Nate to see what is going on. His sparring partner eyes me when Jaden appears from a back room.

“Hey, Giselle.” He smiles. I wave silently.

“Hello Lenora, I see you met Giselle,” Nate says as he looks at me, but my attention is on Lenora. Of course she met me, he sent me there. I roll my eyes.

"Yes, Giselle will help me out with the girls, but I need you to get permission from their guardians since she was so kind enough to pay for the ballet classes for all three."

Nate looks shocked by what she said and looks at me while I turn my gaze to the three special young girls.

"You should have told me, Nate," she says.

"What?"

Cindy interrupts. "I didn't know that you knew a real life ballewina! She showed me this!" Cindy twirls, attempting to perfect what she just learned. I smile at her. The men's gazes are looking at me curiously. Jaden has his mouth open, his eyebrows raised.

Lenora continues like I'm not here. I stay silent, not uttering a word. "That she's a real classical ballet dancer. And very talented, at that. There is only one place she could have learned one of the most difficult Pirouettes and Grande Jete." Lenora looks at me and I meet her gaze knowingly, as she reveals what I have kept from him. "She graduated from Julliard."

Nate's sparring partner's eyes light up as he walks closer and says, "That's like the most prestigious school, it's like the Harvard of dance school."

"Yes, Nick, it is," Lenora says. Nate looks at me, but I won't meet his eyes. I continue to look around, and then Jaden catches my gaze as he stares at me. He looks at Nate and rubs his hands over his face.

"Nate, I need you to contact the girls' guardians so I can get their permission slips on file. I have left them with Charles," Lenora tells him before she turns to me. "Giselle, I look forward to teaching the girls with you. It is truly an honor."

"Yes, Madame," I say.

"I will get them signed, thank you," Nate says.

"Thank you," Lenora says as she leaves.

The three young girls come up and hug me, and I embrace them. The brunette, whose name is Sarah, says, "Can you teach me how to raise your leg like you're doing a split?"

"There are some techniques you must learn first so you won't get hurt, okay?"

"Yes, ma'am."

Nick moves toward me, and Nate catches him by the neck. "Where do you think you're going?"

He is shorter than Nate, but just as muscular, with sleeve tattoos on both arms. He has dark eyes black hair, and looks no older than his late twenties.

"To talk to the beautiful ballerina," he claps back. I blush as I look at Nate, and his face glares at Nick in anger. Nick puts his hands up. "Okay. Okay. I'm sorry, Nate. I didn't know," Nick says apologetically. Nate calms down and looks over at me.

"Giselle, this is Nick, and the guy sitting at the desk is Charles, you know Jaden, and these two knuckleheads behind me are Mike and Sean. This is my team. Everyone, this is my friend Giselle, she will help me with the girls while their brothers are enrolled in our program." They all wave and smile at me. I smile and wave back, meeting Nate's gaze as I try not to get sidetrack by his shirtless body.

Jesus, I need to get a grip on myself. I basically just agreed to pay and teach three young girls ballet and dance while trying to keep my two jobs. He introduced me as his friend, and I cannot lie to myself and say it didn't bother me. One thing I need to tell myself is that sex with him is off the table. I have to remind myself what happened last time and the hurt he caused was like nothing I have ever experienced. It was like it wasn't really him saying those things, but what would I know? I don't even know him on a deep level. We just have this attraction toward each other I can't explain.

Wondering what I should do next, I don't want to interrupt his training more than it has been already. I decide I'll just wait for him to finish. "Nate, I'll just wait over there until you're done."

"Jaden will take you back home," he says. I'm surprised he still doesn't want me here and I wonder what I did that has him in this mood.

I look at Jaden and he nods his head toward the door. "Let's go."

I say my goodbyes to the girls and tell them I will see them next week.

I get in Jaden's sleek, white Porsche, and he heads toward Nate's house. "I'm sorry about Nate back there. He can come across as confusing and moody," he says.

"It's not your fault, you don't need to apologize for him. I can see there is something inside that he battles every day, but he won't let me in."

He sighs. "We all battle something inside, Giselle. We just need to trust the people we are around in order to open up sometimes. I can see that person can be you, and what you did back there for those girls just shows you're a great person inside. I think he was just shocked you did it, but knowing now where you're from changes things."

"What do you mean 'changes things?'" I frown, confused.

"Oh, come on, Giselle. You're a ballerina and he's an MMA fighter. You're from a different world."

"Oh, I get it. I'm too prim and proper now, not a dancer from a strip club. Newsflash Jaden, I obviously cannot go back to New York after my parents died. I left with nothing and cannot expect a spot on the dance company waiting for me with a red carpet. It doesn't work like that. And what does that have to do with anything? I'm from the broke and get-a-job-wherever-I-can world. Help my best friend as she helped me when I was down and homeless. So don't go talking about which world we're from. You know nothing about me or Brie."

When I mention Brie, his hands stiffen on the steering

wheel. "Yeah, well, I know a little about where Brie is from, but let me tell you, Nate and I just don't trust anyone. We may like you, but we don't give our trust and just let anyone in because they wear a skirt and can dance. We've had to earn everything, we come from the gutter raised in shit."

I take in his last remarks and realize how they really see us, and it makes sense in how they are, and if I'm honest, he is right. My parents brought me up in a perfect bubble. They raised me, giving me everything they could so I could live my dream in a different world than they come from. Brie was always with me since elementary school, having a crack addicted whore of a mother who didn't give a shit about her. Still, we try to send money and make sure her mother is not on the street. Hanging out with Brie when we were young, she was bullied for having a mother like that, I was considered a freak that couldn't go to school, they probably thought I was just like Brie's mom since Brie and I were always together.

"Look, Jaden. I'm here as a friend to Nate and nothing else. I will not trap him or distract him. He came looking for me and ask me to come here. Trust me, I was fine," I lie. I wasn't fine, but I was having fun with Jason and Jace hanging out until Nate rode in to whisk me away.

"He has a fight coming up, and he doesn't need to be emotionally drained. I know he brought you here, but Nate is…complicated."

"You know what? I will come and give the classes to the girls, and I will learn to be a teacher, then leave to go to work until the program is over. Then I'm gone." I get out of the car and walk into the house to the guest bedroom. I can't believe him. What the hell is his problem? I pull out my phone and call Brie to tell her everything.

12

NATE

I brought her here thinking I could handle being around her. I can't get her out of my head. I want her and her delicious body in my bed. I know if she sees the baggage I carry inside, she will run. When Lenora figured out where she went to school, I couldn't think straight. A fucking ballerina! This whole time I thought she went to a school and was just a girl who could dance well and was offered a spot at the club for her talents. Never did I imagine she was from that world, a world very different from mine. She paid for those girls so they can dance, the look on their faces like she was a goddess sent from heaven. The answers to their prayers. I know she will honor her word and teach them until the program is over.

She is passionate about her love of dance, it makes sense why she's that good.

I'm no good for her and will just dirty and damage her. I have already begun doing just that. I should have known she went to a prestigious school, and her parents raised her in a bubble. The whole club thing covered it up real nice. She wouldn't understand pain and abuse, how broken and messed up I am inside. How would she look at me knowing what I did, that I let my father get away with killing my mother. I covered up for him and then suffered years of neglect, abuse, and pain, to only end up in foster care with two dead parents; a kid that no one would give a shit about.

All I know is fighting and how to endure pain and inflict it, it's what I was taught and brought up on. How would she fit into my life? The problem is, how do I let her go? I've taken her innocence, dirtied it, and made her feel like she had to clean herself from the possibility she would be pregnant with my kid. A kid that would come from me and a lineage of drug addicts. Why would I want to bring a kid into the world so all he would see is a father who came from a heroin addict and can't sleep in the same bed with his mother.

I see the want in her eyes when she looks at me. I recognize the need. The need that she wants me to dirty her.

I saw the little girls looking inside the dance studio by my gym and I took advantage and talked to Lenora about Giselle. It was an excuse to bring her. I could have left her alone knowing she wouldn't be pregnant or had to explain the burnt scars on the inside of my thighs inflicted by my father. I could have let her be with Bresely, but when I saw him with her at the game or behind her dancing, I saw red.

I have an immense problem when it comes to Giselle. We are just friends, as she eloquently put it. I can't have her, but I don't want anyone else to, either. I know I'm being a selfish asshole and it's not fair, but guess what? Life's not fair, it's a bitch that fucks you.

Jaden comes back from taking Giselle home because I can't train when she is around. I thought having her here would help me calm the demons down. If anything, it made them worse. I just have to deal with it and the need to stick my cock inside her deliciously tight pussy. Looking at her in her sexy leotard inside my gym, a direct contrast to everything I stand for. Even Nick couldn't stop staring at her. I had to tell Jaden to take her home, I couldn't stomach having to look over my shoulder knowing she would be there waiting while men at my gym ogle her. I didn't want to embarrass her further when Lenora laid out her little secret and give her a sweater to cover up her tight leotard outlining her perfect breasts and slim waist.

Now thinking about it, I would like her to wear a Grim Reaper sweater with my name on it. I go into Jaden's office to get a new one from the box he has inside, when I find him already sitting at his desk with a frown on his face.

"What's up with you, brother? Why the face?"

He looks up at me and I know what he is going to tell me next. Whatever it is, I'm not going to like.

"I kind of said some stupid shit to Giselle about her distracting you and being from a different world."

"You did what? What the fuck?"

"I know, man. I fucked up. Even brought Brie into it. Just never thought it would work out. They are both different from what we're used to and didn't want this to impede training and the upcoming fight. She is not what you expected. I saw your face when Lenora said where she went to school. You were shocked, looking at her differently."

I know he is trying to protect us, and what we built. Emotions can get in the way and fuck up everything we have worked for. I can't let that happen, even if I want her more than I should. I can't get mad at him for trying to make sense of all this. We can't get caught up with some girls from a strip club, and I just made matters worse by bringing Giselle here. I wasn't thinking, and it's too late now.

"I get it. I'm not mad, but you should have let it be. I can handle my emotions with my dick. I don't need you meddling in my personal shit, too. Let it go, it will blow over. Once the season in the program is over, she will be done and that will be the end. For now, I will enjoy her company," I say with a smile.

"What are you going to do with the sweater? Isn't that one a little too small for you?"

"It's not for me. It's for her."

He raises his eyebrows. "You want her wearing a sweater with your name on it?"

"Yeah, in here at the gym so she doesn't distract me when she comes inside or anyone else. You saw Nick sniffing like a bitch in heat."

"Whatever. Remember, no distractions. Stop leading her on if your intentions are to not be with her. You're undefeated, Nate."

"I know. Catch you later, brother."

I get in my car and know the shit storm that must wait for me at home. She leaves tomorrow and comes back Tuesday for the lessons to begin. It's not too bad and I at least have her company at the house. I get in my car and drive home. I notice it's silent once I open the front door. I walk through the kitchen to the hallway that leads to the guest bedroom and stop when I see a paper on the counter.

Nate,

I'm sorry I had to leave, Brie needs me to help her out with her mom. I will be back in time to begin the lessons with the girls as promised.

Your friend,
Giselle

Great! I acted like a total dick to her the whole day and can't even make it up to her. I woke up with awful nightmares and didn't want her to see me all fucked up. It was best to just let it pass, and I can take out my anger at the gym. It's the same nightmare lately with my dad waking me up with the cigarettes burns and then slapping to get me up and ready for school, wearing one of the few pairs of pants I had. I had to learn to wash them with a bar of soap and hang dry them. No one would wash my clothes for me and didn't want to go to school smelling like a corpse. I had to figure it out when my clothes smelled, and the older kids would make fun of me. I had to figure shit out quick to survive.

I crumble the letter and throw it across the island. Fuck! She left without calling me and didn't even wait until I came back. I could have taken her or even gone with her, but I know my training comes first. I will just wait until she comes back. I can at least text her to see if she made it okay.

Me: *Hey, I got your note. I would have taken you. Please let me know you got home safe.*

N

I wait until three hours pass and I know she would have landed already if she took a flight, but I keep checking my phone like a love-struck fool. Nothing. She never texts me back.

13
GISELLE

When I called Brie to tell her what happened, she asked me to come down and help her with her mom, and I didn't want her visiting her mom alone at night. Her mom called her, telling her Jack was there demanding money for some drugs she bought, and he needed to collect payment or he would hurt her. Brie told him she would pay him, but to please not hurt her mother, Victoria. Victoria is an addict and is too far gone for help. We have tried everything to get her to quit smoking crack and having to prostitute herself. When I arrive from taking the next commercial flight to Sioux Falls, Brie is already waiting for me to head to her mom's trailer.

"I can't believe you agreed to come, Giselle."

"Of course, you're my best friend and the only person in this world I have left. I can't let you meet up with some drug dealers to pay them all by yourself. How did your mom sound when she called?"

"Strung out, like always, and incoherent. Rambling that if I didn't come and pay Jack, he threatened to kill her."

"How much this time?"

"Fifteen hundred." Shit, that will take two to three weeks to make up, now that I agreed to help Nate with the girls. Fuck it, I still have money from dancing.

"I will pay you back, Giselle. I know we were almost there to open the dance studio like we planned. Now you are going to learn how to operate one doing this for Nate."

"Yeah, he doesn't really know what I want to do in the future. We never talked about it and I think he is just concentrating on his upcoming fight and doesn't have room for anything else right now."

"Did you tell him why you needed to leave?"

"He just knows that I needed to help you with your mom. Not a total lie, but he doesn't know who your mom is and why I needed to come. I don't need judgment or offers for help. You should have seen his face, Brie. When he found out I graduated from Julliard and little Cindy said that it was cool he knew a real ballerina. He looked at me like I was a vase he cracked and didn't know how to put together. He sent Jaden to take me home because he probably couldn't stand me being around him, or at his gym."

"Yeah, probably. It was good to tell him you're just friends to keep boundaries. Jaden and Nate are guarded and don't trust easily. I'm even surprised Nate came to look for you and ask you to help and stay with him."

"I think it's for the best. He doesn't trust me and obviously just wants my body, but not me, the real me he doesn't like, and as Jaden put it, we come from a different world that doesn't know pain."

"Yeah. Whatever. Some people think their pain is worse than others. Try being a girl."

We drive up to a beat up old-looking trailer that has seen better days. It's dark out and we see Brie's mom's old Oldsmobile and a newer model Chevy pickup truck. I'm dreading what we might find inside the trailer. It must smell like death. I remember picking up Brie and she would have to take a shower at my house because her mom didn't clean or have water. She could never keep the utilities on. Brie would take a shower and eat at our house all the time, the only positive thing that I loved about it, was having my best friend over almost every day.

We walk up and Brie doesn't knock, just opens the door to the trailer. Once we're inside, we can see Victoria slouched over, wearing an old top with stains on them and leggings with cigarette burns. The trailer smells like death and something rotten. It hasn't been cleaned in a while. I almost throw up from the rancid stench.

Three men are standing over Victoria, and they all turn, looking in our direction. The one they call Jack is a local drug dealer who everyone knows supplies the crack and heroin in this town. The other two, Rick and Seth, are Jack's little minions, standing on either side of him. Jack is a big man with enormous arms and a belly. He has long, oily hair and a beard that looks shiny and overall disgusting. Seth and Rick are skinny with dirty wifebeaters and stained jeans. The scum of the town, but every drug addict buys from them, even Victoria. Jack has been around here for years and the cops do nothing. He must have them bought because he gets away with everything he does, since I can remember.

"Well, well. Here they are. The town's little princesses." He smiles and I can see his yellow teeth. I am trying to keep calm so I don't throw up.

"Look at you, Brie. And your little friend, Giselle. All grown up. Ain't that right, fellas?"

"Yeah, they're looking hot. I heard they dance at that club, The Porcelain Dollhouse over at Sioux Falls, raking in the cash," Rick says.

"Is that so? Big girls now. Giselle and Brie, two hot pussies twirling on the pole. Hmm." He licks his lips, and a chill goes down my spine. This will not go well.

"We brought you the money so you can leave my mother alone. We will be out of here in just a sec," Brie speaks up nervously.

Rick and Seth move toward the door, and I try not to panic. I look over at Victoria and she is completely out of it, then to Brie as her eyes follow Jack.

"Jack I'm going to give you the money and we are leaving." She grabs the envelope in the back pocket of her jeans, to hand it to him.

He brings his dirty fingers to move his oily hair from his forehead and I notice his eyes are pitch black and evil. He looks at me and licks his lips. "I think I changed my mind and want something more, like your little friend."

"You leave her alone, Jack! She is not part of this. Don't you dare touch her."

He smiles and moves closer, caging us in the small kitchen. Rick and Seth block the door and real fear pools in the pit of my stomach.

"I already had your cunt before and think I want to have a taste of your little friend over there. Her parents are not here to save her and shelter her. There is no one to save you. Your cunt whore of a mother doesn't want you or care for you. Never has and never will. She just uses you to get high and I love to take advantage."

"What is he talking about, Brie?" He said he had her cunt before, it can't be what I'm thinking. No way. Did he rape Brie when she was a teenager? She has never said anything to me about it. I look over at him and he can already sense my fear and is feeding off of it.

"Leave her alone! Jack! You touch her and I will..."

"You will what, you cunt?" He moves fast, raising his hand

and slaps her hard across the face, taking her to the ground. "Rick, hold the little bitch so she can watch! She thinks she can tell me what to do? Now she is going to watch and her little friend is going to get a taste of Jack."

I try to get Rick's hands off Brie and help her, but Seth grabs me and forcefully takes me to the ground. I try to kick but he is stronger than me. Jack holds me with his weight and my eyes burn with tears. He holds his hands over my neck, squeezing so I can't scream.

I look over at Brie and she already has an enormous bruise on her pretty face as blood mixes with tears in her blonde hair. I try to kick Jack off of me because I know he's going to rape me and if I keep fighting, maybe he will get tired. That is wishful thinking on my part and the realization that there is nothing I can do, dawns. I close my eyes as Seth pulls my leggings off, while Jack, with one meaty hand on my throat, unbuttons his pants. I can smell the rancid stench of his breath and body odor. He tears my panties, and I can still hear Brie's muffled scream as Rick holds her from behind, with his hands on her mouth so she can watch.

I know I'm naked from the waist down, feeling dirt on my skin. He pinches my nipples through my shirt, and the pain has more tears streaming down my face. He forcefully slides two meaty fingers inside me, and the pain has me blacking out. I learned quickly that being raped by someone as disgusting as Jack is this one key thing, he wants you to fight back. It's what drives him to keep going. So, I just stop fighting and go limp breathing in and out slowly. One... Two...Three...Four...

All I can do is remember dancing. All the sounds go silent. I can't hear Brie's muffled scream or smell Jack's disgusting breath and body odor. I can still feel his disgusting dick slide inside and I know I'm bleeding from his rough thrusting, tearing my walls over and over and over.

Five…

When I think he's done, he lets Seth come and do the same. Over and over as I lay there, limp.

Six…

I'm bleeding and raw, trying to breathe with Seth's hands around my throat.

Seven…

I'm broken and I will never be the same. If it means dying, then so be it. I have nothing and no one but Brie and cannot let these monsters do this to her.

Eight…

I lie there when they're done.

Nine…

I can feel Brie trying to wake me up. I look over at her with blank eyes. "Oh my God, Giselle!" She is sobbing uncontrollably while her mom is still passed out on the couch.

I try to get up, but blood is running down my legs. I get dizzy and sit up. She scrambles to find something to wrap me in, but there is nothing in the old trailer. She finally finds a comforter in her old bedroom to cover my bloody legs. I can feel the raw pain inside stinging, and I blink back the tears of pain.

She runs to the car and opens the door with tears streaming down her face. She helps me in the passenger seat and nervously turns the car onto the highway to the twenty-four-hour clinic. It's the same one I went to when Nate told to make sure I was on birth control. Funny the first time I went they asked if I had been sexually assaulted. I said no, the first time, the irony. I feel nauseous when we arrive, and I throw up when the car door is opened. I can hear her screaming for help. They come rushing and I'm taken to a room, given sedatives and medicine for the pain when suddenly, everything goes black.

* * *

I wake up in what feels like five minutes, but according to Brie, it's been five hours. "You were in shock. I thought you were dying." She sobs and I hold out my hand to take hers in mine.

"He did this to you, too?"

She nods her head. "Yes, but not this bad, Giselle. He wouldn't stop and kept going and going. Oh God!" She winces and sobs, tears streaming down her face. Her cheek has an ugly bruise forming on her skin that must hurt.

"It's okay, Brie. Don't cry, I would do it again if it meant that he wouldn't do this to you. It's not your fault."

"Yes, it is. If didn't call you to come with my mom, this would have never happened."

"No, it would have happened to you alone and you could have been left there for dead. Your mom was out of it and didn't even know what the fuck was going on." My voice is scratchy and my throat is raw and sore as I begin coughing, trying to speak, pissed off at her mother.

"Shh, Giselle. Calm down." I look at her.

"Promise me you will tell no one about this."

"I promise, no one has to know."

"Please, Brie."

"I promise."

I'm discharged with a lot of medication they give for rape victims. I'm lucky that there wasn't enough damage that I can still have children. Doesn't matter though, who would want a child with a girl like me? I was basically gang raped by a disgusting drug dealer. I'm damaged, worthless, and broken. I wince, still feeling the pain between my legs as a reminder that it wasn't a dream. It was real and it will haunt me forever and I know I will never be the same.

Dealing with the pain through painkillers, Brie still thinks it's a good idea for her to stay at my apartment. I've woken up in cold sweats every night for the past two nights, screaming for someone to get off me. Brie is there, watching me, crying myself to sleep. She holds me and rocks me back to sleep every time they come, the memory playing in my head.

I have to go back on Monday to begin the lessons as promised on Tuesday. I continue to sob in Brie's arms. "I can't hear them, or you screaming for help, but I can still feel it burning, and I want to throw up. When I wake up, I can't breathe," I whisper.

"The therapist at the clinic said you will have these types of episodes. Like PTSD..."

"I know. I just want it to go away, Brie."

"In time, it gets better. Maybe going to Vegas and teaching the girls will be good," she says as she hugs me close.

"Yeah, but I don't think I can look at Nate the same, ever. I feel dirty and don't want him to touch me or anyone to touch me. I will teach the girls, but I will come home as soon as Thursday and dance at the club."

"Are you sure? So soon, Giselle? You just..." she trails off. I know she means well, but dancing is all I have.

"Yeah, I'm sure." I sniff and look at my phone, not realizing that I had a missed text from Nate. I open the message and it says he wanted me to call him when I landed. I laugh to myself.

"What?" Brie asks.

I show her my phone with the text message, date and time.

"Oh, Giselle. I'm so sorry."

"Too late now," I say, placing the phone on the bed and getting up so I can get my suitcase and have Brie take me to the airport in the morning.

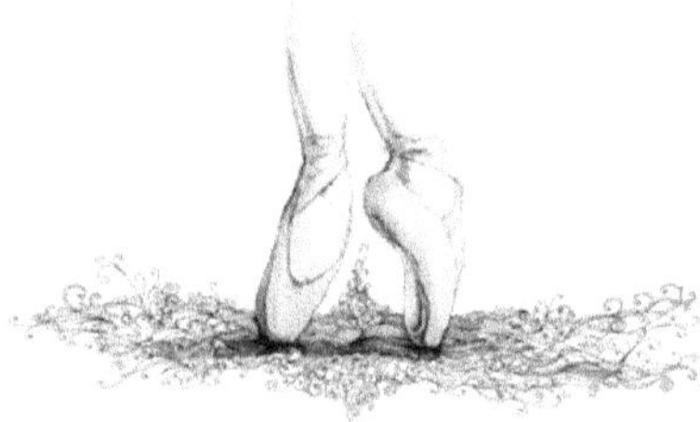

I wake up the next morning, and the pain has subsided significantly, but the pain within is a different story, I feel empty, my soul lost and broken. It screams in pain, for me, and for my best friend.

I will go back and teach the girls the love and art of ballet. It's all I have left inside. The only thing they didn't take away is my love for music, dance and ballet. The chance to be seen, without looking inside.

I take a cab from the airport to Nate's house, I arrive around dinner time, knowing Nate goes to bed early. I have to wear a hoodie and anything that covers my neck. I found a turtleneck bodysuit to cover the deep purple, and blue bruising around my throat from anyone to notice. Brie and I found a perfect foundation for my neck and her face, that will work, but if you're sweating, then not so much. I scan the driveway and see he has people over, including Jaden. Brie was going to come with me, but her face needs a bit more time to heal. I walk up and knock on the door with a suitcase in hand. I wait about five minutes and the door opens and its Jaden.

"Hey, Giselle. The team is in the theatre room looking over the last fight. You're welcome to…"

I don't look him in the eye and interrupt his invitation. I have no intention of accepting.

"That's okay, Jaden. I'm tired from the flight and I just want to go to bed. I need to wake up early and get to the dance studio. Nate likes to get to the gym early in morning."

"Giselle, are you okay?"

"I'm fine, just tired." I walk into the hallway toward the guest bedroom and leave him standing there with the door open.

Closing the door behind me, I decide to lock the door, so no one can open it while I'm taking a shower. I hope Nate doesn't come and knock. I quickly lay out my outfit for the next day with a hoodie and high-neck bodysuit. I check making sure the door is locked again. When I am satisfied, I take a shower, and go to sleep praying I don't wake up screaming in cold sweats.

I decide to lie face down and have as many pillows as possible. Maybe that will help to muffle the sound in case I wake up screaming.

In the middle of the night, I wake up in cold sweats, and look at the time in my phone, 4:59 a.m. It felt like I couldn't breathe again, rubbing my neck that still feels sore, but not too bad. I decide to take a shower and get dressed because going back to sleep is not an option. Carefully looking over my thighs, you can see the bruises are not as bad. I decide to wear black stockings until the marks are gone. I check the time, 5:59 a.m. I decide to open the door, dressed in my hoodie and leggings over my pantyhose to the kitchen.

I find Nate sitting, drinking his morning shake, eating eggs and fruit. He smiles when sees me. "You're up early. Good morning."

"Good morning," I murmur. I don't return his smile and I avert my eyes so he cannot see the look on my face.

I take a yogurt I bought at the airport out of the fridge for breakfast. I grab water and sit at the other end of the island and scroll through my phone.

"I texted you the other day." I stiffen.

"I was kind of busy, sorry." I continue to scroll through my phone searching for basic ballet positions you can teach beginners at a young age.

"Giselle, are you okay?" he asks.

"Yep. I'm fine, why?" I answer him without looking up from my phone.

"You seem like, I don't know, something's wrong."

"Nothing is wrong." I look up and give him the look I have felt every day since that night. Lost, broken, without a soul, and screaming inside.

He looks at me trying to find the Giselle that left who the other day, the one who felt an unrequited love. What he doesn't know is that Giselle is dead and gone. The Giselle he is looking at, the one no one will want, is just a shell that can only dance to be seen.

"If there is something wrong, you would tell me, right?"

"There is nothing to tell. Don't worry about me, Nate. You worry about your fight, and I'll teach the girls, as promised."

"I want to repay you for the tuition for the girls, it's a lot and…"

I hold a hand up, stopping him from speaking.

"Don't worry about that, Nate. I can dance and make up the money. I wanted to pay for it, and don't expect you to repay me or give me anything. I'll just dance like I did when I made the money."

He gets up from the chair and startles me. "I don't want you to dance for anyone like that!"

I smile sarcastically. "I guess I will work it off at the diner. Either way, I don't want your money. I'm your friend, not your girlfriend, and I don't belong to you, or anyone."

"I told you, you're mine."

I laugh. His face turning serious. "Oh, Nate, I can't ever be yours," I scoff.

"Your too good for me, is that it? The prima ballerina," he snaps back.

I give him a murderous glare. "You know nothing about me!"

He rubs a hand over his face taking a deep breath.

"Look, I'm sorry if I hurt you. I didn't mean..." he trails off.

"There is nothing between us, Nate. I just want to be friends. I'm no good for you, and you're right, I'm a prima ballerina. Teach the girls the ballet lessons, lessen the load with Lenora, and I will leave. I will go back in between the lessons because I don't want to distract you from your fight. Jaden is right, you need no distractions." The last parting shot, I knew, would get him to back off. I know how much he cares about his career as a fighter, and I don't blame him. I know how it feels to only have one way out, to sacrifice everything for what you have built.

"Okay, fine. But this isn't over."

I roll my eyes and grab my bag. I wait for him so we can head out.

We arrive in the parking lot, and I walk toward the dance studio, leaving him there, without a word. I open the dance studio and let out the breath of air I was holding in. Lenora gave me a key, since I would be here early, to practice some dance routines. It's the first time I can practice since they raped me, and I decide it's the perfect time, where no one is watching me. I play Evanescence's *Breathe No More*, and I dance, bleeding from my soul, shedding my pain, so no one can see what's been taking me under every night. The tears slide down my face, as my soul screams in pain. Broken, lost, and undone. I dance, remembering the free spirit I once was, allowing the tears to fall.

I breathe and when I'm done, I realize I'm not alone.

I look over, to find Nate, Jaden, and his entire team standing there, silent. Nate walks up to me slowly and wipes the tears from my face gently with his thumb.

"Who hurt you, baby? You can tell me," he whispers. I stand back looking over his shoulder at his team, knowing he would do anything to protect them. The same I have done for my best friend. They did this to her, and she lived with it, a secret she never shared, even with me. I know why now, the shame and pity. I can't ever tell him what happen to me. I look at Jaden, remembering his words about pain.

If he only knew Brie has been living in pain. A pain that I felt all at once, a sacrifice I would do again, if it meant that she wouldn't have to go through it, even though she witnessed it happen to me. Jaden stares right back and he knows pain, seeing it in my eyes, and looks away. Nate stares at me as I look down, not wanting him to see.

"When you're ready, I'm here." I nod, turning to dance to the next song, *My Immortal*.

I don't care if they stand there, I can't right now.

They stay and watch me bleed my soul; for me, my friend, my parents with every jump and twirl, the loneliness that will soon follow, even after I scrub my skin raw in the shower, trying to remove the filth I still feel crawling on my skin until there is nothing left but pain. It's a feeling I'm getting used to, one that is part of me, reminding me of what was taken.

They eventually leave when I'm done. Shortly after, the kids walk into the studio, I smile, and act like there is nothing wrong. The young girls are excited, and it gets me through the day, to see their captivated faces as they learn something new. I give them extra time, as I feel the love for teaching young girls' ballet.

I put the hoodie on to see if Nate is finished training, knowing it's boiling out, but can't risk anyone seeing the bruises until they heal. I walk with the girls to the gym and see Charles seated in the front. He smiles, welcoming me.

"You must be Nate's girl. Giselle, right?"

"My name is Giselle, but I'm not Nate's girl. I'm just a friend."

He snorts. "Deny it all you want. You're his girl."

I inwardly sigh. I look over at the cage and see Nate sparring with Nick. Jaden comes out of the office, probably noticing that am here from the surveillance cameras.

"Ready to take me to the fort?" I ask sarcastically.

"No, I actually think you should stay."

"I don't think that's a good idea."

"What happened, Giselle? I called Brie and she won't pick up my calls, or texts."

"Nothing happened. Can you take me back now, or should I call a cab? Don't want to distract the champ."

"Fine. Let's go." I can hear Nate call Jaden's name.

"Yo, Jaden!" I see Jaden turn and wave him off. Once we are in Jaden's Porsche, I stare out the window as he drives me toward Nate's house.

"Giselle."

I sigh. "What, Jaden?"

"Back there earlier, you dancing like that. We all saw it."

"Saw what?" I ask through clenched teeth. He pulls over and looks at me.

"The pain you're in, the tears streaming down your face. Brie not answering. What the fuck, Giselle? Tell me if you will not tell him. Either way, we will find out."

"There is nothing to find out, so good luck. I'm from a different world than yours, remember, Brie and I? We don't know your pain. There is nothing to find out, so do yourself a favor and leave me the fuck alone. Just drop it, please."

"Whatever it is, you know Nate will do anything for you. You know that, right?"

"There is nothing he can do, Jaden. I have to get back to the club for my shift and meet Brie."

"Okay, I will take you to the airstrip. You and Brie are taking our plane from now on, and will be driven to your place, or work until you come back for Thursday's lessons, with Brie." I close my eyes not wanting to argue.

"Fine."

I agree because I know he will go sniffing to find out what happened, and need him to drop it. I fall asleep and lock the door to the guest bedroom when we arrive at Nate's house. I hear Nate when he knocks on the door, but I don't answer. Giving up, he leaves for his room.

I arrive the next day in Sioux Falls and, as promised, a driver is waiting in a black Bentley to take me to my apartment. The driver tells me he is going to wait for Brie and I until we are ready to go for our shift.

I meet Brie in her apartment, ready to head out.

"Jaden is pressing me about what's wrong with me. I could finally dance, and they saw it, Brie. Nate was patient and wanted me to open up and tell him what was wrong. I can't Brie, ever." I sniff.

"We don't owe them anything. He called and I didn't answer because I knew he felt something was wrong. You can act like nothing happened, but not after what I saw them do to you. It was worse than what that son of bitch did to me," she says as a tear rolls down her face.

"Today we dance together on stage instead of alone, okay? Like we practiced. I will tell Jake to play Evanescence's *Lithium*. We will get on the pole and go down like we rehearsed."

Brie nods. I knew she would like to try the new moves I practiced with her, anything to make her forget. When we arrive at the club, it's more crowded than normal, but we think nothing of it. We get busy waiting tables and I'm wearing another high-necked leotard with black fishnets to hide the bruises. Since it's dark, you really can't see Brie's face with the marks across her cheek and her lip is not as swollen as the day I left. We head out, passing our table section and a hand shoots out, grabbing mine and entwining their fingers with mine, and I jump, startled. I look over and I see Nate frowning at my reaction.

"It's me. It's okay."

My eyes widen in shock. "How did you?"

"We took the next commercial flight," Jaden interjects, looking at Brie, frowning. She notices he is trying to see her face if the marks are a trick of the light.

I save her from answering. "It's great you guys are here, but we really need to get ready. It's our turn to go up and Jake is about to call us."

"Okay. We'll be right here." I smile, but it doesn't reach my eyes.

14
NATE

I had to come and see her. She wanted to leave and be here with Brie. Something happened to Giselle. I know deep down it's bad. Jaden told me she said "good luck," in us finding out. Jaden has been looking into why Brie is avoiding him. I saw the marks even if he didn't, someone did something to them and when I find out who, or what, they will see the wrath that will be unleashed. The DJ announces Giselle and Brie's stage names, and I look over my shoulder to the regular tables, and notice three guys from the wrong side of town. They smell of old stale cigarettes. A smell that reminds me a lot of where I grew up. The song plays and I see the girl that I'll do anything for, dancing in a high-neck body suit. Weird, she would wear the same type of clothing, except this one had sequins on it. Brie is on the other side in a similar position, and I suddenly hear the heavier set guy in the back speak. I catch what he says about the girls, but it's what he is says, that has Jaden and me stiffening.

"Yeah. There they are, my two pink pussies twirling on the pole for daddy Jack. Remember, Seth, how she just went limp when I was pounding into her tight cunt over and over? She tastes even better than her friend. Her momma was so high, she didn't know what was going on." He laughs and I see red with rage. Jaden and I get up from the table and I grab the fucker by the neck.

"What the fuck did you just say, motherfucker?! You did what?!" I yell through clenched teeth.

He laughs as he grabs my hand from squeezing harder, making his eyes bulge. Security is coming from the entrance, and with no choice, I have to release him. I don't want to cause a media showdown having this spread like wildfire through the internet. People look over, and pull out their phones to record. I point my finger in his face.

"You're dead, motherfucker." He laughs, getting up and leaving, but not without one last nasty remark that has me seething in blinding rage.

"Oh, come now. 'The Reaper' and his manager have a soft spot for town pussy. Hey, even Seth got a taste, while her friend watched," he bellows with laughter.

I rush him again, and Jaden holds me back. "Chill, Nate. We will get him, just not right now," he says, breathing deep.

"That motherfucker raped her, he fucking raped her," I say through clenched teeth, trying to avoid anyone from hearing what I'm saying.

"Get her records from that clinic, Jaden. ASAP." She must have gone to the same clinic across town. I look at her while she's dancing, and it all makes sense now. The tears, the fucking pain she must be in; that motherfucker broke her. I can't see straight with all the rage coursing inside me. I can't even sit still while my leg twitches, waiting until they come back. What do we even say to them? I look over at Jaden and he's on his phone. He looks up. "Don't tell them we know. It won't go well, you know they will shut us out. We just take them back with us, and deal with it at home," he says.

My leg is shaking so badly with rage, I need to calm down.

Jaden is right, it's not like back in the day where I can just fuck someone up and kill them.

The girls come back over, and I see my girl with her lost soul. The sparkle is gone and has been replaced with sorrow and pain, gutting me. I will do anything to take it away. Those assholes are dead. She won't even look at me like she used to, with want, and fire in her soul, needing me. She flinches when I touched her, standing away from me when I get near, and locks her door to the room when she sleeps. All the signs were there, and I was too stupid and full of myself to notice. That disgusting pig raped them. I will find him and his little minions, and when I do, I will end them.

"Let's go. We need to get going."

"Okay, let me get my hoodie and we can leave," she says.

They leave to get their stuff and I get an incoming text from Jaden with an attachment. I open it, and find Giselle's medical report. Jaden looks at me while I scan the attachment. "It's a 24-hour clinic. It's not good, brother. He fucked her up bad."

I look at him, and I see the sadness on his face. He read it. I look at it, not being able to wait. What I read is the worst thing I can stomach. Internal bleeding, tearing, contusions on her neck and body, nipples and chest area. She needed a blood transfusion from the loss of blood. It shows she can have children in the future and was treated with pain medication, antibiotics, and for any diseases as a protocol for a rape victim. Two different, unknown males raped her while one held her, choking her. She came into the urgent care unit in shock, in and out of consciousness. She was treated for over five hours, and sent home. That's why she couldn't text me back. Instead of me going after her and making sure she was okay, she was being raped, while Brie was assaulted and forced to watch.

He has raped Brie before, like he said, laughing, and I know Jaden is looking into it. We wait patiently until they come back with Brie, sporting a fresh face of makeup. We don't look at them, or make any comments.

On the plane, Giselle is in a corner with her knees tucked under a sweater. I get up, and sit next to her. "Are you cold, baby?" I breathe. I don't want to freak her out by touching her. She turns to me, and I raise my hands so she can come lean on me. I will do my best not to touch her, and just hold her gently. She nods and leans into me, and it's like heaven, to smell the sweet scent of her hair. I breathe her in and lay my hands to the side as she falls asleep. When we are almost about to land, she wakes up in the airplane, screaming in panic. Brie rushes from the back of the plane and takes her from me, rocking her.

"Shh. Giselle, I'm here. It's me. They can't hurt you," she whispers, and I look at them in shock.

Similar to what I go through every night, except no one is there to rock me. Jaden stares at them like he's seen a ghost. A ghost he is familiar with. The captain gives the signal that we are landing, and I kneel to pick up Giselle to take her back to the seat. Brie looks at me and I can see the bruises now that she's closer, and I look at Jaden. He looks at her and gives her his hand. She takes it and sits next to him placing her cheek on his shoulder.

We get to the house, and I take her to the guest bedroom. "I'm sorry I had a nightmare, it was nothing," she says softly.

"I know what happened."

Her eyes widen. "What are you talking about?" she says defensively.

I show her the medical records from my phone as I hand it to her. She slides down the bed and I kneel next to her. "Look at me. They were there tonight, and I can't keep that from you. I'm going to kill them, do you understand?"

Her eyes look into mine and she shakes. "You can't. It changes nothing, Nate."

"You think they can just get away with it and let them walk, like it's all good? They were laughing about it and I am not sure they won't try it again. I threatened them, but I showed restraint, and restraint to people like that, they confuse it with weakness. I can't let you go back there, or Brie. You're not safe there. Predators will wait and won't stop after they taste what they can't have freely. Brie will stay with Jaden and you will stay here. We will figure this out. You're not okay, Giselle. What they did… I read the doctor's medical reports."

I close my eyes with rage simmering inside at what I want to do to those assholes. I want to rip them apart limb from limb, to inflict the pain they have inflicted on her. She gives me back the phone, not wanting to look at the pages that remind her of what her body went through, reliving what they did to her physically. Mentally and psychologically, she's in pain. I know what damage feels like, what pain feels like, and being powerless to make it go away, or seek revenge.

"Giselle, I'm going to take care of you, and you must trust me. I would never hurt you. I'm going to help you."

"How? I'm damaged, Nate. I'm a porcelain doll that is broken, and even if you try to put it together, it's never the same. I will never be the same. I can't sleep. My skin feels raw from me scrubbing the filth that won't seem to go away. Sometimes I can still smell them, and I just want to vomit. They should have just killed me," she whispers.

"Don't say that. I get it, and you never have to worry. No one will do this to you ever again. You have my word. I will protect you, Giselle."

Meaning every word, I will protect her, and I will kill those motherfuckers who put their hands on what's mine. Jail is not good enough, not in my book. I could easily get them arrested, but for what? They will be set free, and then they will come after them again. They're scum drug dealers who feed addicts, preying on young women who come from those sides of the tracks. They may have broken her, but what they didn't know was that she belonged to someone who was born from their world. Who is just as fucked up with a dark soul, who only knows pain and how to inflict it. They don't know that the Reaper is going to come and collect. Right now, I'm going to put back together what they broke and damaged, something that belonged to me that is delicate was touched by me, and only me.

"Let's get you bathed and to bed, baby," I whisper into her hair. I get her up and walk her to my room. She stiffens when I place my hand on her lower back. "I will not hurt you, trust me," I say softly.

Running the bath, I undress her slowly. Making sure I don't freak her out or touch a part of her body that is tender or sore, knowing I need to help her. She is like a fragile piece of glass you're trying to piece together but can easily come apart in a million pieces, and then you have to start over. I remove the high-necked leotard and peel it off slowly over her head as she raises her arms. When it's completely off, I hold my breath when I see her neck, angry with bruises, purple, and blue wrapped around her delicate skin. They are in the shape of two hands that gripped her so tight, it's a miracle she is still alive and breathing. That asshole was choking her, while he was raping her, so she wouldn't scream. I look down her legs and between her thighs, more bruises of fingers, and hands where they were holding her legs open. My eyes fill with moisture. I have never shed a tear since I watched my lifeless mother on the floor beaten and battered by my father's hands, while I silently cried, peeing my pants, looking through the crack of the doorway from my room. I blink so she can't see the tears in my eyes or the rage inside me of having to wait to seek my revenge.

They touched my girl. They fucking broke her. All they left was a shell and a battered soul. I place her in the bathtub and slowly use my hands to clean her skin with the softest touch. I want my touch to be the one she feels washing her clean of the filth she keeps feeling. She stares blankly at the wall and stays silent, and I know she is screaming inside. I know what that pain feels like when you feel you have nothing to live for. I wash her thoroughly, slowly, and when I get to her neck, I give her soft kisses and wash her, as she doesn't move or flinch. She just sits there, empty, and I hope she can feel my touch and my caress. It's amazing she can still dance, she must be taking the painkillers they gave her.

I let her go to the dance studio, getting my bag out the trunk of my car, not wanting to argue with her. She was so closed off and I wanted to give her space, but I heard the music so profoundly. I had to at least catch her dancing even if, at the time, I thought she was mad at me for how I treated her, or for what Jaden said to her. My team was waiting, and followed me into the dance studio, and what I saw there had me almost to my knees. Watching her dance so passionately with the pain that was radiating from her with tears falling on her beautiful face. I knew it wasn't what I did. I knew she was shattered and broken. Someone had taken something from her that couldn't be replaced. My team saw her pain, Jaden and I recognized it, and knew what it felt like. Her soul lost and broken, screaming in silence, as she danced in sorrow, broke me. My ballerina was broken. I felt powerless, and I knew in that moment that someone damaged her. She didn't need to say it or tell me that someone hurt her. It was there, in the song, in her dance, in her movements, and her silent tears glistening down her face. My team witnessing it all, none of them could look me in the eye after she continued, after I wiped her tears.

Thinking back when I made it to the gym, after witnessing her dancing in sorrow, Jaden assured me he would find out what happened. He was as determined as I, knowing what it felt like. The pain that comes from a shattered soul, the fucked-up kind that never makes you whole again. When she looked at him, he saw it in her eyes, the pain and sorrow even when he tried to tell me that everything would be fine. "It's probably not that bad," he had said, but we both knew that was bullshit, as he uttered the words from his mouth.

I dry Giselle and dress her in one of my white T-shirts and place her in my bed. She doesn't protest, just lying on the white sheets, staring at the wall. I quickly shower and slide in next to her, wearing boxer shorts. Usually, I sleep naked but I don't want to freak her out. Wrapping my arms around her and breathing in her sweet scent, I close my eyes.

"I have nightmares, too," I whisper. I know she can hear me because her breathing changes when I speak.

"No one knows except Jaden. It's why I don't sleep with anyone in my bed, why I'm alone in this cold house. You're the first I have allowed to be my side. I've woken up in pain every night since I was a child." I kiss her temple softly and hold her, hoping she can hear me and understand the reasons for my behavior. The reason why I shut her out.

I'll be here waiting for her nightmare to come, because I know she is just as damaged as I am. One thing she isn't, is alone. I close my eyes, ready for the demons waiting, but what I have now that I didn't, is a reason. Something I didn't have before… Her.

15

GISELLE

I wake up and I don't remember where I am at first. I can feel a warmth on my back, a hand circling my waist, and my memories come back. Nate bathing me, dressing me, and taking me to his bed. Falling asleep with me after he told me he had nightmares since he was a child. That I was the only person he has slept in a bed with, promising me that he would keep me safe, and let no one hurt me. Can I trust him? He said I was his before then he rejected me, sent me away, told me to make sure I didn't fall pregnant, dismissed me, and finally hurt me. He says one thing, but does another.

It shouldn't matter now, I am just a broken soul living in a shell of a body, invisible and damaged. Who will want me with all my emotional baggage, anyway? It doesn't matter. I don't matter, he can treat me however, and I won't care. I feel disgusted, raped by two men polluting my insides with their nasty cocks cumming inside me over and over, after they had their fill. Who will want me when all I can remember is their nasty hands bruising my body, tearing my insides, the feeling of agony, my body in pain, blacking me out of consciousness, counting until I could come back, and when the pain was excruciating, the blackness would take me under, suffocating me along with Brie's muffled screams.

Remembering the smell of the trailer and stale cigarette smoke from Jack's breath makes me want to vomit. I get up and run to the bathroom, dry heaving as the memories come rushing in, trying to empty the contents of my stomach, but there is nothing, just saliva stringing from my mouth. Suddenly, hands are grabbing my long hair, pulling it away from my face, and holding it. I can feel Nate rubbing circles on my back with his hands. "It's okay, baby, let it out. I'm here."

He helps me off the floor to the sink to brush my teeth, the mint of the toothpaste welcoming as the scent fills my nose, replacing the memory of the horrid smell. I brush my teeth and I realize that all my toiletries are in his bathroom.

When he feels I can stand on my own, he leaves me alone to get ready. I stay silent and close the door, locking it, needing a sense of security. I know he is stronger than me and if he wanted to, he could do whatever, and no one would find out. Nate is quiet and can be cruel, but he isn't a rapist. When I danced privately for him and I told him to stop, he stopped and didn't demand or force himself on me. It's silly that I locked the door when I just woke up from the same bed we slept in, but I can't take a shower taking the chance of him seeing me scrub my skin raw. I need to feel the pain the scrubbing of my skin provides, so I can feel.

After a while, scrubbing my skin, the pain that ensues feels raw, tender, a need to feel alive. I'm on the shower floor after scrubbing, using a small hand towel to do the job. I would have honestly preferred a scouring pad, that would have sufficed, but I couldn't find one. Nate knocks on the door and when I stay there for a minute or two, he picks the lock and opens it, to find me on the shower floor with my knees bent, and my head resting on the tiles.

"Giselle?" I just lay there with the water falling on my face, and don't answer. "Look at me baby, please." I turn my head and see his muscular thighs in his shorts, but I don't look up to meet his eyes. He shuts off the water and carries me in a white, fluffy towel that is so soft, or maybe it's because my skin is red and tender. "You're going to have to trust me, I am going to touch you, okay? It will help, but you have to look at me, and know it's me." I nod.

He unwraps me after I am dry, and I lay there naked as the day as I was born, not caring if he can see all of me because it doesn't really matter. He turns my face as he hovers over me, and I can see the tattoo on his neck that goes up the side of his close-shaved scalp. The tattoos on his knuckles caresses my face, and I don't flinch or stiffen. His touch is soft and my skin tender. The sensation is welcoming. A thumb rubs my lower lip as he lowers his mouth and kisses me softly. I don't move while he continues to kiss my lips, sliding his tongue inside, opening my mouth, and seeking my tongue. My eyes find his and he slides his hands up my face as he breaks the kiss. He places soft kisses down my neck and goosebumps follow his wake. He kisses every bruise on my skin, trying to replace the hurt. "I want you to remember me, and only me on your skin," he breathes.

He kisses me everywhere and when I look down, he is not only kissing me, but he is memorizing every mark on my body that was brutally inflicted. I watch the emotion on his face as he takes them all in, and I know he is picturing how they raped me, piecing it together. I lay there watching him, feeling his touch on my skin. I know he needs to get to the gym to train, his fight only three weeks away. The ballet lessons for the girls begin again tomorrow. I can at least dance in the studio since Lenora gave me a key. I can go with Brie if Jaden brings her along.

When he kisses me one last time, I look into his eyes, and I see the promise of tenderness and protection that I'm not sure of. He may not physically hurt me or rape me, but he can still inflict pain in other ways. I need to keep in mind that he is a different monster.

He helps me up and opens the closet, coming back with expensive dance outfits I don't recognize. They all have tags on them in my size with matching dance socks. I look up at him and he says nothing. He places a hoodie on the bed that has his name with the Grim Reaper on it. "I got you a hoodie that you can wear over the dance outfits so you can cover your neck, and no one will see the marks. I was supposed to give it to you before you left because I wanted you to have it."

"I don't care about the marks. I wore the jacket with the hoodie so the girls wouldn't see or anyone at your gym. I couldn't stomach them thinking you did it. I have heard horror stories of fighters..." I trail off.

"You didn't have to, everyone knows I wouldn't touch a woman, especially you. I appreciate you worrying about me like that. It shows you are selfless and that you care, even in pain. Thank you."

Staying silent, I get dressed, not caring where the clothes came from, and wear the hoodie.

We eat breakfast and arrive at the gym. He ushers me inside and Charles smiles welcomingly. "Your friend is in the office with Jaden," he says.

I look over at the office door, and it opens to a running Brie. She runs toward me, stopping right before running into me, and slowly embraces me. "I missed you," she whispers.

"I missed you, too."

"Are you okay?" she asks.

"Yeah, I think so."

"Are you girls going to stay and watch me train today?" Nate asks.

"After I go practice with Giselle, we will stay and watch you train," Brie says.

"Okay, but Charles has to go with you." I raise my eyebrows, looking over at Charles.

"Ready, Charlie? It's okay if I call you Charlie, right?" I ask. He raises his eyes to Nate.

"Nate's girl can call me whatever she wants."

"Charlie, we've been through this. I'm Nate's friend," I say.

Nick comes up behind Nate. "Nah, you belong to Nate, and your friend Brie belongs to Jaden. They never bring girls to the gym," he says as he winks.

"Whatever."

"Where did you sleep last night?" he asks. I avert my eyes.

"Exactly," he says knowingly, with a smile on his face.

"Leave them alone," Jaden chimes in, giving him a death glare.

"I'm just trying to help," Nick says.

Charlie follows us to the dance studio as I play Lana Del Rey and practice moves with Brie. I decide to show her the dance moves for the ballet lessons tomorrow. Charlie sits and watches, fascinated by the intricate dance moves.

When we finish, he walks us back to the gym, and I can see a crowd around the cage while Nate is sparring with Jaden. I have never seen Jaden fight and he's actually really good, as he holds his own against Nate. They move, circling each other, and suddenly, Nate goes for the takedown, but Jaden moves faster, and kicks him back against the cage. Nate recovers and goes after Jaden, measuring his distance, until he finds a weak spot, punching Jaden and taking him down. When Jaden is down, he grabs his neck with his arm from behind, and Jaden suddenly taps out.

"You're faster," Jaden says. "It's good that you're faster. The asshole you're fighting will not know what hit him. I bet he doesn't know how fast and calculating you really are."

I heard he is fighting another fighter from Brazil, thinking he has a shot against "The Reaper" for his title. He goes by the name of Maverick De Leon. His father is from Brazil, and his mother is French, according to the promotion on TV.

Nate sees me through the cage and blows me a kiss. I stay stunned, not knowing what to do or say. Everyone looks in my direction, waiting for a reaction. All I can think of is to stay still. It's all I can manage, feeling guarded inside. I look over at Brie, gazing at Jaden, following his every movement. I look at Nate and I can't blame her; they have bodies carved like statues, perfect in every way. The sweat dripping down their bodies has any woman buying a ticket, but not to watch them fight. Men built like them break girl's hearts. They do not mend their shattered souls. I might have a hard time trusting Nate, but what choice do I have?

I will never be the same again. I'm used and tarnished, like a plastic bag with a gaping hole that can't be used. When Nate is done, I say my goodbyes to Brie, Jaden, and his team. He comes up behind me, placing a hand on my lower back. I look over at him, and he smiles. "When we get home, I want to take you somewhere."

"Where?"

"It's okay. Trust me, you'll see."

"Okay."

We get inside his car, and he drives to his house. I secretly liked when he said 'home,' like it was my home too, but that's a lie. I'm just here because we can't go back until he takes care of Jack and his minions. I think he will just hurt him, but killing him? I don't think he will go that far. Could he?

Maybe he is just saying that in the heat of the moment. I can smell his cologne as he showered in the gym, and he smells fresh, like the hoodie he gave me. It smells like his cologne and I feel like I am being hugged in a cocoon from something he gave me that has his name branded on it. Like I'm part of him, belonging to him, because as fucked up as I am, I prefer to belong to Nate "The Reaper" Phoenix, even if he can't love me.

No one can love me, so it doesn't matter. Love is not on the table anymore; no white picket fences, no relationship, or a boyfriend to worship me. That shit doesn't exist for a girl like me anymore. The prima ballerina is broken, ruined, and can only dance to shed her bleeding soul. To be visible when I dance is better than wishing death because, to be honest, I have thought it better to have died instead.

It's quicker, painless, and I don't have to see the pity in anyone's eyes when they find out two trailer trash drug dealers that had been waiting, raped me. I remember what Jack said about me being around Brie, that he finally could get to me, too. The evil look in his eyes promising me pain. He broke me, giving me pain all at once, like the death of my parents, alone, with no one capable of helping me, not even Brie.

They followed us to the dance club and if it wasn't for Nate and Jaden, they could have done it again to finish the job. I owe Nate that much. He saved me by giving me a safe haven. When we arrive in his driveway, he parks his white sportscar and opens his garage to a sleek, blacked out super bike. He hands me a helmet and a pair of Bluetooth headphones to pair with his phone. I watch him take a helmet and place one on over his headphones and pull the bike out, revving the powerful engine. We secure our helmets in place, the headphones linked so I can hear him speak through the headset inside the helmet.

"Hold on to me tight and don't let go," he says through the speakers.

"Okay," I say.

He gives me a hand to get on the bike, one leg over, and I slide as close as possible, circling his waist, feeling is ab muscles contract. He revs the engine and rubs my hand laced at his waist as he closes the garage, and rolls the bike slowly through the gates.

"Ready?" he asks through the speakers.

"Yeah." I hold on, my chest tight against his back in excitement. He plays *Bring Me to Life* through the headset and the bike takes off down the open highway, like a bat out of hell.

My adrenaline spikes as the exhilaration of the wind and lights pass me, giving me tunnel vision as the bike, Nate, and I move together like we are one thorough each turn at breakneck speed. I have never felt so free, so alive, like nothing else matters but this moment. The adrenaline coursing through my veins feeds me, the higher level of my consciousness, and the pain my soul bears. I've felt nothing since the night I was shattered.

He pulls off to a place that sells burgers and it reminds me of a place back home where high school kids would hang out. The place is full of college and high school kids. Everyone looks over at us on Nate's bike because it's so loud.

When he parks the bike on the side, he gives me his hand, so I can get off first. I take my helmet off, careful not to drop the headphones. I decide to undo my braided hair and let my hair fall in waves. He gets off the bike and takes his helmet off. People whisper and take out their phones to record us.

"Yo, that's Nate 'The Reaper!'" one kid says.

"What's up?" Nate says back. He turns to face me. "Did you like it?" he asks.

"I loved it! Thank you." He smiles and takes my hand so when can get in line to order some food. I didn't realize I hadn't eaten, and my stomach rumbles in protest. People let Nate and I move to the front of the line to order, recording us with their phones. They begin bombarding Nate with questions after he orders us food.

"Are you ready for the fight, Nate?"

"It's sold out."

"Is that your girl?"

He rolls his eyes, turns around, and holds my hand.

"Yes. To all of it," he says, speaking loud enough so that everyone can hear.

The young college girl's fire back, "Well, at least your girl is beautiful. So, it makes sense.

"What's her name, Nate?"

I look around blushing, not used to all the attention. I forget that fighting is huge in Vegas, and Nate is a pro fighter.

"Giselle. My girl's name is Giselle," he says. The girl at the counter gives him our food as she giggles. I roll my eyes. I can't believe he's telling everyone recording with their phones that I'm his girl. We both know I'm not his girl. He just feels sorry for what happened to me, and he is helping me out as a friend. I don't care either way, I'm no one. What do I care what they think? We sit next to his bike while people photobomb us while they take pictures. We eat in silence, Nate removing all the carbs from his meal as he watches me eat.

"It's good," I say.

"Best place in town. I thought this would be good for you, a change of pace."

I look at the bike.

"I loved riding with you," I say.

"You weren't scared or tensed up on the turns like I expected you to be. I was surprised. I found something else we both enjoy together. It works." He looks at me, and I know his words have a double meaning. He can't mean sex, that was before they dirtied me and tarnished me like dirty water. He must be disgusted by the thought of even touching me. I look away.

"Is it always like this? The attention?"

He nods his head. "Yeah, everywhere I go. Get used to it, now cameras will follow you wherever you go."

I look at him, not believing what I'm hearing. Now I know why he brought me here, to the busiest place in town. Makes sense. He wants the cameras to follow me. It's why he said I was his girl. How clever. He planned it.

I don't know if I should feel happy, or disappointed. Maybe I liked the thought of being his girl, to be known in the world as Nate's girl.

We get up from the outdoor tables and he pulls me in for a kiss, and I let him. He's trying to help me, not hurt me. I owe him that much. He kisses me so deep my toes curl. He doesn't care if everyone takes pictures or records us. He slides his tongue inside my mouth as he sucks my lips, tasting the hint of the chocolate chip cookie I just ate. He slides his hands on my waist, bringing me close, and I can feel his hard erection against my belly.

"She really is his girl, judging by that kiss he just gave her," one guy says to our right, breaking the spell the moment cast upon us. I was completely lost, letting him take what he wanted, but I know I won't deny him.

We get on the bike and head back to the house. He speeds through the highway with the music feeding the adrenaline, once more relieving my pain.

We get inside the house feeling exhilarated and he guides me toward his shower. I strip and stand under the hot spray, grabbing a fresh washcloth to scrub my skin. Nate walks in and his hand shoots out, stopping me, naked in the shower. I look at him in all his naked glory, from his muscled chest to the deep V defining his abs down to his cock.

"Not tonight, baby." He washes me clean down to the apex of my thighs that are not as tender, sliding his fingers, washing my pussy and ass gently.

Turning me to face him, I slide my hands slowly down his body, feeling all of him. He walks me back to the shower wall and gently kisses my neck where the bruises are healing, fading like a rainbow. I stand there letting him as I crave his touch. He slides his tongue down to the bruises on my breast, where they pinched me on my nipples, he kisses and sucks on them gently.

I let him have my body because my soul is lost, and my heart is nowhere to be found. He continues down to my pussy as he kneels, raising my leg over his shoulder. I can't believe he would want to lick my pussy, but I let him. I don't care and it doesn't matter. His tongue strokes my lips and slips inside my folds. I mewl when he sucks on my clit, swirling his tongue, and my pussy gets wetter. The water slides down our feverish bodies, making my nipples hard. I raise him, and it's my turn to return the favor. I kneel in front of my protector, licking his dick from the tip down to his balls, tasting all of him. I remember what I saw in the back room, mirroring everything, and taste the saltiness of his pre-cum when I suck the tip of his dick. He runs his fingers in my hair fucking my mouth slowly at first, but then I pick up the speed sucking harder, faster, taking his huge cock inside my throat, relaxing my neck muscles so I can take all of him inside my mouth. I continue to suck, twirling my tongue up and down the shaft of his dick.

"Fuck, baby, that feels so fucking good," he grunts.

Holding himself, bracing the wall with his arm full of tattoos down to his hands, while his other hand is holding my head steady as my head bobs, sucking his dick like it's the lifeline I need. He pulls his cock out, turns the water off, quickly dries me in a towel, and carries me to his bed. He lays me down and settles between my legs. I open them wide, and he holds my face with his while he hovers over me with the tip of his wet cock at my entrance.

"I'm going to make love to you, Giselle. I'm going to take it away," he whispers on my lips. I lie there and just look into his eyes, lost. He can try, but it won't change anything. The damage is done and I feel I owe him for protecting me. He slides into me slowly, stretching me inch my inch and the pain I thought I would feel is instead pleasure. He continues to slide inside me, feeling my wet pussy.

"Are you okay?" I nod, keeping silent, closing my eyes. "Don't close your eyes. Look at me, Giselle. It's me, baby."

I open my eyes sliding my hand on his face, kissing him

deep, and slide my tongue devouring his mouth. Tasting my pussy and his dick on my tongue, he moans inside my mouth, making his dick harder inside my pussy. He pumps in and out slowly, sliding his hands under my ass so he can drive his cock deeper inside. I wrap my legs around his waist as he grinds his cock inside me while his balls slap against my ass. I moan as the pleasure intensifies, our tongues inside, fucking each other's mouth. He breaks the kiss and looks down into my eyes while he maintains a slow pace. "God, you're so beautiful. You will always be mine, Giselle. Always."

I listen to his sweet words I beg are truths. He told me I was his before, but he sent me away. He rejected me when I questioned how he got the scars, but guess what? I have hidden scars inside me, but at least he knows where they came from. I don't know his pain, only the pleasure he gives me, and I fall to the most intense orgasm I have ever felt. I scream his name as I cum, my pussy gripping his cock. His eyes close as he cums, spilling his hot seed. He pulls out a minute later and gets a wash cloth to clean me gently.

He wraps his arms around me, bringing me to lie on his chest. Right before I fall asleep, he whispers a confession that gives me some peace, "I don't have nightmares when you sleep with me." It is the last words I hear before sleep consumes me.

* * *

The next morning, I wake up, stiffening when I remember I had sex with Nate last night, but it doesn't matter, it's the least I can do when he's been taking care of me. I didn't have a nightmare last night, but it doesn't mean I won't. It's happened before. When I think they're gone, the next day, one would come harder than the last, laughing at me like I'm a bitch. I turn around and see his back turned. Needing his warmth, I turn over and slide my hand around his waist until I reach his chest, spooning him while his heat radiates from his body, warming me. I feel his breathing change as his hand slides over mine, holding it there, and I fall asleep all over again.

That's when it comes; the feeling cold, being unable to breathe, the squeezing of my throat, the smell of the stale cigarette breath, my worst nightmare coming back to claim me, I bolt up the bed with a piercing scream, gasping for air and look around. I'm not in the trailer, but in Nate's room, and he isn't here. I turn my head toward the bathroom and the door swings open with a bang.

Nate runs to the bed, water dripping down his beautiful body and a towel around his waist. "Shh, I'm here, baby. I'm here. You're safe. No one is going to hurt you ever again," he says softly. He holds me, rocking me, turning my head into his wet shoulder, shaking as tears slide down my face, I stay silent and wish that I was better off being dead.

He kisses me on my tear-stained cheeks, my eyes, my neck, back up to my lips, and it feels so calming that I stop shaking. I look at his face, the pain I feel mirrored in his gaze, and relieved it's not pity because I can't handle pity. It's what he must have thought went I asked him about the burn marks, and he sent me away defensively. I wasn't pitying him. The old me wanted to know how he got them. I wanted to know Nate, the real Nate. Now I'm too fucked up to want anything but pain on my skin to cope with the sorrow that's inside.

I get up and take a shower, leaving him on the bed. I take the washcloth to scrub my skin, but I pause, dropping it. I finish washing myself, turn the water off, and dry myself after hearing him moving around in the bedroom.

I walk over to the floor-length mirror, knowing what I want, and what I need. He walks up behind me in his gym shorts without a shirt and looks at me standing naked through the mirror. He is so much taller than me, over six feet, and his massive frame makes me look fragile. I reach behind me and grab his hands slowly toward my stomach, sliding lower to the wet folds of my pussy, and I close my eyes. He slides his finger inside and my pussy clenches around it. My heartbeat races.

"I want you to fuck me hard, Nate. I want to watch you pound me in every fucking hole in my body. I want it raw and hard."

"You don't know what you're asking," he breathes. I open my eyes and look at him with determination as I raise my brow.

"Are you saying no?"

"No, I'm saying that I will not be gentle. I don't want you to think that I'm like those pigs who hurt you."

"There is nothing you can do that can make me think, for a second, you're like those fucking monsters."

"Bend over and touch the floor, straighten your legs, and look at the mirror," he says.

I do as he asks, trusting him. He bends his head to look at my exposed ass and shaved pussy. He pulls his shorts down and he slides his cock forcefully inside me while he grips my hips hard. The pain his cock is inflicting is a welcome pleasure as I watch him bite his lip while he pounds into me. My knees almost buckle, but he holds me, sliding in and out. He slides his finger inside the puckered hole of my ass with the pressure of his cock inside of me, pleasure mixed with pain, and it makes me feel alive.

The pounding of his huge cock feels like my insides are tearing. I like it, and I want more. Watching him fuck me over and over, I don't even want to cum, getting off on the pain he is inflicting.

He notices and looks at me in the mirror, moving us over to the bed. He lays me face down on the edge and holds both my hands behind my back to keep me still, and I let him. I let him fuck me raw, hard, and fast. I widen my legs, standing, jutting my ass to give him better access to my pussy, and he slides in, balls deep. I moan, reveling in the pleasure, and pain. I push my ass back while he slams into me.

From this position, I can still see us in the mirror as he fucks me raw like a caged animal not holding back. When he finds his rhythm, my pussy clenches around his cock, milking it.

"Harder. Fuck me harder, Nate." His cock swells, pulsing inside me, and I know he is on the brink of cumming. He pulls my hair around his hand.

"You like to watch my big, fat cock fucking you."

I moan.

"This pussy is mine and I'll kill anyone who touches it," he says, looking at the pure lust and desire in my eyes through the mirror, knowing his cock is causing both pleasure and pain, and that it's him inflicting it, branding me, and making me his.

He pulls out, turns me on my back, and holds my legs open, with my ass on the edge of the bed. He looks down, admiring my open pussy ready for his plucking. He slides his finger down, the wetness dripping toward my ass, coating it, slipping it inside my tight hole.

"Next time I'm going to pound this sweet ass. You'd like that, wouldn't you?" I look into his face, reaching for his thick chain around his neck, and bring it close to mine.

"Yes," I whisper.

His eyes turn black with pure lust, desire; a monster inside unhinged and waiting to feast. He licks my neck, slides his tongue into my mouth while his cock slides in and out of my aching, swollen pussy. I bite his lip, drawing blood as he fucks me faster and harder while the metallic taste of his blood drips on my tongue.

"Cum for me, baby. I want you to cum all over my cock while I pound your sweet pussy," he says against my mouth.

I didn't think I could cum, but an orgasm builds inside me, gripping me, taking me over the edge, and I moan as he continues to pound me harder. When I cum, he pounds into me hard with a deep thrust, and my pussy floods all over his cock as I moan his name.

I open my eyes after the stars have cleared. His eyes are closed while my pussy pulses. He pulls out, drops to his knees, and eats my pussy, sucking all my juices down to my ass. He sucks and sucks until I am completely clean.

He continues to suck and eat my pussy. He hooks my legs over his shoulders, sucking my clit. I scream in pleasure, pleasure he can only give and I cum hard on his tongue. He raises his head and when I think he's done, he stands, his erect cock jutting out, and he slides it inside, fucking me in and out.

"Your pussy taste so good," he says while watching his cock slide in and out the folds of my pussy wrapped around his thick shaft.

"Hold on, baby," he whispers.

I nod. He slams into me, looking into my eyes. His thrusts are deep, powerful, and I cannot lie, my pussy is raw and sore from him fucking me. I have never felt so alive. He thrust into me one last time. I grab his ass, pushing him deeper into me, while his cock spills his hot cum inside, heating my raw flesh. When he pulls out, there is blood mixed with cum on his cock. He frowns and raises his head with a worried look. "Did I hurt you?"

"No, I'm fine. I promise. I needed it."

To ease his mind, I push him off me, and when he stands, I slide to my knees and grab his still-hard cock in my hand. I suck on it, cleaning the blood mixed with both of our cum, his eyes close, holding my head steady as I take him completely inside my mouth to the back of my throat.

I keep licking and sucking his cock all the way to his balls. He groans when I slide my tongue back up around the head of his dick, and lick the last drop of his salty cum. I slide my mouth off with a pop.

"Your cock is delicious." He smiles as he raises me to my

feet, kissing me, feeling the bite mark I made, and the taste of blood on his broken skin. He can taste us inside my mouth and it's the most erotic experience. I pull back breaking the kiss. "I'm sorry I bit your lip."

He smirks. "See, and I thought I was hurting you."

"There is nothing left to hurt," I say, as the light goes out of my eyes.

I get up and walk toward bathroom to take another shower. My pussy is so sore and raw, I think I'm going to be limping. One thing is for sure though, Nate has an enormous cock. I wasn't thinking it through when I agreed for him to fuck me hard in my virgin ass next time, but at least he didn't find me all weird with sex. He doesn't look at me with disgust and whatever I ask of him, he gives.

16
NATE

I watch her go, leaving me standing there watching her walk to the shower. I feel her pain. The worst part about it is that she wants more pain to feel alive. I know what living like that is like. I do it every day. It needs to be fed, if not, I prefer not to go on anymore. When she asked me to fuck her hard, I almost didn't give in. I couldn't live with myself if I hurt her. I vowed to put her back together. I shouldn't have shut her out, putting distance between us, but that was before and this is now. Even after they broke what's mine. I still want her more than ever. It's better that they won't see me coming. They think they got away with what they did to her, that no one will care or do anything about it. They're wrong, and I will make them pay. I will come and collect. They just don't know when, but I do, because no one touches and breaks what's mine. She says she has nothing else left for anyone to hurt, and the funny thing is, I believe her. She wants me to give her pain mixed with pleasure. I live in pain, inflict it, and receive it in the cage. The pain I'll give her is the pleasure she doesn't know she desperately needs. I'll fuck her hard, leave my hidden marks, branding her, and make her mine.

We eat breakfast and drive to the gym. She has lessons for the girls in the afternoon, so she will hang out here with Brie until it's time. Lenora took a vacation since Giselle was staying with me and not going back to Sioux Falls like we initially planned during the week. It relieved me when she asked if Giselle could cover for her. When we enter, the big televisions I have placed in the gym have the sports channel on. Everyone stops and listens to the reporter on TV talk about my upcoming fight, and then it shifts to a more interesting topic: My personal life. I close my eyes because, deep down, I know they have reports about Giselle and me on the bike. I did it on purpose in a way, so that cameras would be on her. I want those assholes to know she is constantly being watched when she is with me.

The reporter continues her story with the entire team watching, Giselle stops and looks at the screen with a worried look on her face. Brie and Jaden come out of the office also transfixed on the screen, listening as a video clip shows me kissing her at the burger place with all the teenagers and college kids recording, replaying the part when I stated she was my girl, that we're together. When I think that is all, I hear the reporter continue with video clips from her dancing on my lap at The Porcelain Dollhouse in her sexy outfit with the black lights glowing on her body while I touch her. I stiffen, never thinking that anyone had a video of her dancing there, as more clips of her sliding down the pole, stopping inches from the ground as celebrity athletes throw thousands of dollars in the air for her. One guy raises the volume to hear what the reporter is saying on TV.

"Giselle Monroe, a recent graduate from Juilliard, is the new love interest of the popular pro MMA fighter, Nate 'The Reaper' Phoenix. Apparently she is known to dance at The Porcelain Dollhouse, and reports are saying she has only ever danced personally for him.

Don't get too excited and show up at the dance club in Sioux Falls to get a show. Fans at local Burger drive in have seen her in Vegas on his motorcycle, if anyone can judge by the video clips sent in. Sorry ladies, the rumors are true.

One interesting clip is the one that shows how talented Miss Monroe really is, as she is a classical ballerina and choreographer. The interesting couple have taken social media by storm, being the most searched couple on the internet in the last two days. An anonymous fan sent in a video of her performing at Juilliard. Let's take a look."

I continue to look at the screen and a professionally edited video shows off her dancing to her favorite artist, Lana Del Rey's, *Young and Beautiful*. Her ballet outfit is impeccable as the passion on her face describes the art she is painting in ballet slippers dancing on pointe. She moves with grace, performing her turns and jumps I have only seen in professional pictures of famous ballerina dancers, but she certainly is beautiful, and a genuine artist as she moves with the music. I can see her soul. I look at my team, Brie, and Jaden, mesmerized by her movements as she glides effortlessly. Brie has tears sliding down her cheeks as she sees her best friend in all her glory, delicate and beautiful, moving across the theater with her dancers following her.

Giselle stands motionless, stiffening, and looking at her phone. She receives an incoming text and I see Brie doing the same. They both look at each other as Giselle wipes Brie's tears and they both say name 'Dean' at the same time.

"Who's Dean?" I ask.

They both widen their eyes, not noticing me looking over at them.

"He went to Juilliard with Giselle. He's a talented editor, but went there to be a conductor for the orchestra. He used to record all of Giselle's performances," Brie says.

I don't know why, but I'm fucking jealous of Dean. He's seen Giselle perform and I have only seen tidbits from the club. The closest I have seen her dance ballet is when she is bleeding her soul in the dance studio.

Giselle turns to me. "He texted us saying he gave them that video. He didn't want them thinking I was some wannabe Julliard graduate dancing in some club," Giselle explains.

Nick and the guys turn toward me from the cage. "Yo, Nate. Your girl is a bad bitch. I can't believe she's Money Monroe. So she must be Coco." Nick points to Brie, smiling.

I give him a murderous look rubbing my hands down over my face. The guy has the potential to go pro, but he gets on my nerves with Giselle. I stop Jaden from going over and punching him in the face while the other guys look at Giselle like she's a goddess.

"Alright, I know I got carried away, but you two are like a famous couple right now. They love her, the Ballerina that dances for the Grim Reaper," he says, with his hands up.

Great. That's where the media and fans are going with this. Fine. I can deal with this in a positive light. I turn to Jaden. "She can't go anywhere alone with Brie, they will recognize her and paparazzi will be all over them. I don't want them scared, but phones record everything."

"It's not like you don't go everywhere with her anyway," he scoffs.

"If you don't want me to fight outside of the cage on camera, then do what I ask, brother."

"Fine."

"I need to concentrate on the fight and then we have to take care of our little problem afterwards," I say low so no one can overhear our conversation.

"I got plenty of information, just need some time for things to die down. This asshole you're fighting keeps talking shit on social media, so I need you to not let him rile you up. You know he's going to get to you through her, just be mindful, and don't lose your head."

"Whatever, motherfucker gets out of line, goes near her, and he's done." Meaning every word, I know I'm being overprotective with her, but I have a burning rage inside like the devil in Hell waiting with his demons because of what happened to her, and I feel somewhat responsible. I let her go alone, and they broke her. Even in death, my father left demons behind trying to take away anything good. It reminds me of how I failed my mother. I let my father get away with her death. Even if she was a junkie, she didn't deserve to die. My father died quickly and painlessly. My mother was battered, her face beaten and disfigured. She didn't deserve that. He did, now they're both dead, and I can't do shit about it. I live with the guilt that I helped him, stayed quiet, and took his abuse. He died, but he left his demons to torture me every fucking day of my life. The only person who makes the nightmares stop is Giselle. When she is with me every night, by my side, in my arms, even when her nightmares come, I'll be there waiting to fight for her, reminding her she is safe. She's my reason, a reason to feel alive even if it's through pain.

I train all day and I'm the last one to leave. Brie popped in and left with Jaden an hour ago. She said Giselle was still in the dance studio with Charles. Charles is a nice man with a big heart. He lost his daughter and wife awhile back, needed a job, and I gave him one. I think he sees Giselle like a daughter. He doesn't mind that I told him to stay and watch over her and Brie when they were in the dance studio. I trust him even when I give him shit about him telling Giselle that we are together, and not just friends, playing the matchmaker. I don't even know what we are, but friends are not what I would call it. Girlfriend, maybe. I've never had a girlfriend. I've only fucked girls and sent them on their way because I'm not capable of letting anyone in. I'm fucked up and I know it. I don't know what love is between a man and a woman. I've never experienced it and I don't think I'm capable of it. Women see me as eye candy, an opportunity to be with a multi-millionaire pro fighter to buy them designer purses and shoes. To be seen with me. When I was broke, I had nothing but street fighting to pay for my next meal. Yeah, they were down to fuck, but that's it.

I close up the gym and head over to the dance studio to pick up Giselle. When I open the door, I find Charles transfixed, watching her dance on pointe in her ballet slippers to the sounds of the piano. *Even in Death* by Evanescence echoing in the background, as the voice and her body sways to the rhythm of the music. It's like watching an artist painting a blank canvas. She dances in pirouette in a gothic grandeur to the ballad, its haunting and beautiful. She's all dressed in black like a dark version of a ballerina. Charles turns to me as he hears me walking, noticing me when I opened the door on high alert. He has a pistol that no one is aware of as he continues to watch her.

"That's for you, Nate. You can feel it pouring out of her, the life and death of love. It reminds me of the way I love my wife and daughter. In life and in death. Your ballerina dances for you."

"Thank you for watching over her for me, Charles. I can't repay you enough."

"You can, by doing right by that girl. She needs you. She's in so much sorrow and in pain. I have been watching her for hours, but to her, I'm not here. I don't know what happened to her and I'm not asking you to tell me. This is all she has to cope with whatever she is feeling. Her eyes are soulless except when she looks at you. You're her anchor, her chain from falling deeper into the depths of whatever she is feeling. I'll see you tomorrow, champ." He gets up from the chair and heads toward the exit.

"See ya, Charles."

I walk up to the dance floor, and she notices me but doesn't falter. I stand motionless in the center as she bends and twists a single leg up. I try to not reach out and touch her. Her hand comes up and softly slides down the side of face. We look into each other's eyes as the lyrics of the song continue. Charles is right. She dances for me and it's the most beautiful thing I have ever seen. I pick her up, she circles her legs around my waist, and I kiss her chest softly, holding her close. I walk us back against the wall on the other side of the mirror to hold her back as leverage. I pull her leotard down and gently kiss her beautiful breasts. She looks down as her breath quickens from the pleasure. She slides down my front, my erection is hard against my shorts, and I know she can feel how hard she makes me. Her hair is in a messy bun. It releases from the confines of the band as I tug, letting her hair cascade down around her shoulders. I kiss her softly. I want to take her right here, but I prefer her in my bed, where I can take my time. Tonight, I won't take her hard. I'll give her pleasure at softening her pain.

"Let's go home," I tell her.

She nods, expecting me to tell her more. I can see it in her eyes, but I can't. I'm rendered speechless by her beauty. Her dancing seared in my memory, for me and only me. She lights me on fire. I want to burn with her and only her. She is the light to my darkness, and I am the darkness to her light.

17
GISELLE

I never thought he would watch me dance. I was dancing out my feelings for him, feelings that have grown deep inside my shattered soul, trying to make sense of the need I have for him. The need of pleasure and pain only he can give me. I thought he would say something, but I sometimes forget its Nate. He doesn't love or do emotion, he's closed off and private. I don't know what demons haunt him because he won't tell me. I am convinced he never will. So, I will hold on to the lifeline he gives me, his pleasure mixed with pain that I crave, to continue to live another day. I am nothing more than a shell; a body for him to keep his demons at bay while they feed off mine. It's okay, I don't matter anyway. Trading one monster for another won't matter, because either way, I'm lost and alone. He makes love to me after we shower in his bed. I go through the motion and enjoy it, but I won't look into his eyes. He senses me withdrawing from him, not physically, but my soul is lost, and in his darkness, I can't find my light.

The rest of the week is the same, except he doesn't watch me dance. I give the ballet lessons and wait for him. I talk to Brie, and she catches me up on town gossip. Jace reached out to her and Jaden wasn't happy. She told him they were just friends. Jason asked about me, hoping I was happy over here, and to let him know if I needed anything. If he only knew there is nothing he could do for me; I'm damaged, lost and shattered with too much emotional baggage that he doesn't need. He deserves someone better that is not fucked up like me. Brie knows I am not okay, so she hides the fact that isn't either. She was there, it haunts her, and she feels responsible. I keep telling it wasn't her fault. If she went alone, they would have killed her, and I couldn't lose my best friend. I have no one else that is like family. She hasn't spoken to her mother, and the last she heard was that Jack has been staying in the trailer, most likely waiting for us to return to finish the job. I'd rather die than have them rape me again. They should've killed me, and I sadly wish they had. I keep having nightmares. Nate is there, holding me, and rocking me. Tears I once had stop falling. It's just the screams and the feeling of not being able to breathe that gets me. Nate's fight is five days away. I keep to myself so I don't distract him. He has been training at the gym and even at home. I leave him working out in his home gym and work on the next lessons for the girls, watching videos of techniques. I want to get new dance outfits for the three of them. Lenora could only supply two, but they have worked so hard. Brie agreed to come along so we can pick some out at a dance store close to the area. I think if I ask Nate, Charlie will come along, and it would be okay. I spot him coming back to the room from his work out

"I wanted to ask you something, if that's okay."

He looks at me while I sit at the edge of his bed with his white, expensive sheets, my feet on the grey lush carpet underneath his massive king-sized bed. I clasp my hands together in my lap. I'm wearing a black T-shirt with my scrunchy socks on.

"What is it?"

"I wanted to buy the girls new dance outfits tomorrow.

Lenora only gave them two, and they have been working so hard. I wanted to go with Brie and Charlie, if that's okay."

He looks hard at me. "No."

"Why?"

"Because it's crazy with the fight. People will take pictures and bother you with questions about us. Remember, at the burger place, how everyone was?"

"I didn't ask you to tell them I was with you, you planned to do that all on your own and you didn't bother to ask if I was okay with it," I retort.

"You didn't object, either. You didn't deny it, you played along. I did it to keep you safe. You need to have eyes on you, so they don't go after you, or Brie. It won't be safe until after the fight."

"Is that the only reason?"

Secretly hoping for a different answer, he closes his eyes, and inwardly sighs. When he opens them again, the words that come out are not the words I expected.

"Yeah, that's the only reason."

I should feel hurt like before, but I don't. Deep down, I expected it. There really is nothing he can hurt me with. I look up into his eyes, expressionless.

"At least we are clear on that. Don't worry, I'll order it online." I get up and leave his room.

"Where are you going?"

He looks panicked, reaching for my hand.

"To be alone, I want you to leave me alone." I step away, walking down the hallway to the guest bedroom and I lock the door once inside. Getting in the bed, I close my eyes, but the tears don't come. I don't have any. I'm empty. When my eyes close, the demons are waiting to consume me.

I wake up not being able to breathe, bolting upright in the bed. I place my hands over my mouth, so he doesn't hear me scream. My soul screams in silence as I shake uncontrollably, alone in the dark bedroom. I lie there awake, afraid to close my eyes, and wishing I was dead like my parents. The sun streams through the window and I've lied awake the rest of the night. I don't have lessons with the girls, so I stay in bed, not wanting to see Nate. I hear a knock on the door a short while later.

"Giselle?"

I stay silent.

"Giselle, I'm heading out. Just tell me you're okay and I'll go."

"I'm okay. You can leave now."

He stands there as I can see the shadow of his sneakers under the door for a while. Suddenly, he walks away, I hear his retreating footsteps and the closing sound of the front door. I hear the garage door open, then the engine of his motorcycle roaring and speeding down the highway.

I try to get some sleep, but the nightmares come back. This time I can hear Brie screaming to stop, and then a muffle. I hear the beating of my heart and the smell of Jack's rancid breath on my face, telling me that my pussy is so tight. I run to the toilet in the en suite bathroom and dry heave. I notice its 10 a.m. and I haven't eaten breakfast or drunk any water. I quickly shower, scrubbing my skin hard with a washcloth, feeling relief from the pain. My skin is raw, probably with a burn rash, but I'm past caring. The bruises on my neck are completely gone. I decide to wear a long-sleeve crop top and low waist skinny jeans. I tie my Doc Marten boots and my hair in a messy bun and apply makeup to cover the dark circles under my eyes. Saying to myself in the mirror, "Fuck it." I decide to doll myself up with heavy makeup, spray perfume, and head to the kitchen. There is a note from Nate saying to open a manilla folder. I open it, I find a key fob, and the papers with the title of a brand new Bentley in my name. I stand there shocked, not believing he bought me an expensive car. Opening the front door, I walk outside to the Versace driveway. There is a shiny brand new black Bentley SUV with red brake calibers and black rims. I walk to the front of the car, admiring the beautiful black paint. I have never owned a car before. I notice the front license plate with a Grim Reaper on the front. I inwardly smile, opening the car door and sliding in the driver's seat, smelling the rich leather permeating the interior of the car. The leather feels so soft underneath me, I look at the rearview mirror glinting in the sunlight, and there is a necklace with a ballerina wearing a tutu covered in glittering stones. I touch it, feeling excited about having my car. I pull out my phone and there is a text from Brie.

Brie: *You must have received your gift as I did, I'm waiting for you with Charlie at the valet entrance to the dance store.*

I smile, texting her back.

Me: *Yes! I will be right over.*

I decide to text Nate and thank him.

Me: *You didn't have to buy me a car. I would have taken a cab or an Uber. I'm not being ungrateful, it's beautiful. Thank you for understanding.*

Nate: *You are welcome. Any issues, call me.*

Me: *Okay.*

I lock up his house, grab my purse, and head toward the

dance store. I get to the front, seeing Brie and Charlie waiting for me to arrive by the valet where the stores are located. It's an exclusive store for dancer apparel I found online and I can't wait to get inside.

"Wow, I thought the Porsche I got was nice, but holy shit, is that a Bentley?" Brie says.

I give the keys to the young valet driver, and he can't stop staring at me. "You're the Reaper's girl? Giselle?"

My eyes go wide. I almost deny it, but I would just look stupid. Nate will make it look like a breakup after, anyway.

"I guess, for now," I tell him.

"Well, if he doesn't want you, then there are plenty of guys waiting for him to fuck it up. You're gorgeous, and the way you dance is awesome," he says, turning red.

"Thank you, I think." I get the ticket he gives me and walk toward Brie and Charlie.

"What was that about?" Charlie says.

"Nothing, he recognized me. I almost denied it, but what's the use? I would just look stupid. He did it to calm people down and protect me. It's not real," I say, lowering my voice as I shrug my shoulders.

"He said that?" Charlie says angrily.

"Yep."

Brie rolls her eyes, shaking her head muttering under breath while we walk toward the store.

"Nate is an excellent fighter, but dumb as rocks when it comes to you."

"It's okay. Charlie, I'm no good for anyone, anyway."

Brie's steps falter as she looks at me with concern and sadness.

"I'm okay, really. I'll be fine. I really want to get the girls the outfits. They will be so excited. I think I'm going to buy them one for every day of the week they have lessons," I say excitedly, changing the subject about me and Nate.

When we are in the store, word spreads like wildfire that I'm here, and suddenly, there are so many people around me. I can hear the questions being thrown at me. Am excited about the fight? Am I worried? Is Nate ready? Are we serious about being together? Honestly, I want to laugh really hard at the last one. 'Serious' is not what I would call it, more like fuck buddies getting their rocks off on some twisted shit. I ignore it all, concentrating on picking out the sizes, while Brie gets the ballet slippers and dance shoes. We are both smiling while Charlie sits and waits on the red velvet sofa in front of the register. I admire how cute all the outfits are, especially little Cindy's outfit. I feel a looming presence in my peripheral vision, watching me. I turn as I place the items down at the register. The cashier, a young girl with glasses, pink dyed hair, smiles at me, and looks over with wide eyes. There is a large, muscular man, maybe two inches shorter than Nate, titling his head in my direction.

"Hello. You must be Giselle. I have heard a lot about you, *Hermosa,*" he says in his slight Brazilian accent.

"That must be Spanish, or Brazilian. Am I right? I don't know what it means exactly, but how do you know my name?"

He smiles with straight, white teeth and has tanned skin. He has light eyes and is very attractive, but definitely not my type. "I'm Maverick, by the way." He sticks his hand out and, not to be rude, I place mine in his. He slowly bends and kisses the back of my hand softly. I immediately pull my hand back. I can see Charlie come up with a pissed off look on his face.

"Leave her alone, Maverick. You know Nate and how this will go down. This is low, even for you."

"Aww, come now, Charles. I was just introducing myself to the beautiful young lady. You know how Nate is with women. It would be a shame for him to treat her the same way he does with the others. Just recently, he was in the back making out with the one with the big breasts who wanted his autograph after his last fight."

My stomach drops at the mention of his last fight and the woman he must have been intimate with. He just gave an autograph, maybe held her waist, but I thought that was it. My face must have lost all color because Charlie looks at me, worried about what he sees. I realize why they asked the question about us being a serious couple. I must look stupid, but I don't care.

The guy named Maverick looks over at me and frowns. "I'm sorry to have upset you. Please forgive me, I was out of line. Look," he turns to the cashier, "everything she wants in the store is on me."

A look of shock replaces my face and I move quickly to stop him from handing the cashier his card. I place my hand on his.

"Please don't. It's okay, really. You don't have to. I don't know you... I—"

"It's okay, Hermosa, I was wrong and offended you. I apologize and I insist on paying." The cashier charges his card and hands me the receipt, placing the items in the bag with a big smirk on her face.

"He's fighting Nate, Giselle. He's trying to beat Nate for his title," Charlie says. I see Charlie's murderous glare at Maverick.

"Is that right? So, you go up to all the women Nate's with and introduce yourself?"

Brie nervously takes the bags.

He chuckles. "Oh no, beautiful. Just you," he says, looking me up and down appreciatively.

I'm done with this conversation and annoyed by him. "I gotta go. Nice meeting you, Maverick."

I walk toward the exit of the store, leaving with Brie and a fuming Charlie.

"Giselle?" Maverick says and I turn my head back.

"What?" I ask sarcastically.

He smiles, his eyes the color of the ocean against his tan skin. "I love the way you say my name." I roll my eyes and continue out of the storefront.

Phones are recording our little uncomfortable conversation, pictures are taken, and someone requests his autograph. The man has a colossal pair of balls to even approach me. He wants to get under Nate's skin, it's obvious, I can't forget what he said about Nate, and the way he is with women. We walk in silence and wait for the valet to bring our cars. A crowd forms at the valet area with phones flashing, taking pictures and recording. I tell Brie and Charlie we'll see each other at the dance studio. I get in the Bentley, my phone rings, and it's Nate. The Bluetooth picks up the speakers echoing his breathing. "Had a nice time shopping today?" he asks sarcastically.

"Yeah, it was actually better than last night. Why?"

"We need to talk when you get here. See me at the gym."

"Why?" I ask.

"Please, just do it."

I sigh. "Fine."

The call ends. When I arrive, I park in the lot in front of his gym next to his motorcycle. I walk inside and Nate is in the cage going at it like an animal. Nick is taking forceful blows but blocking them with protective gear. I stop in front of the cage as everyone stops to look in my direction. I forget that I'm wearing low-waisted skinny jeans and a crop top. I must look out of place inside an MMA gym full of mostly men. Nate stops and stares at me, looking me up and down. He opens the gate of the cage forcefully and some of the guys jump back out of his way. Staying rooted to the spot, my eyes take in his bulging muscles, his flat stomach, his abs flexing as he breathes fast, in and out. He looks furious as he stops in front of me and takes his mouthpiece out, sweat dripping down his neck.

"You said his name, touched him, and then you let him pay for all the outfits for the girls," he says menacingly.

"First, I didn't know who the hell he was. I didn't touch him in the way I'm sure they made it seem. I was stopping him from paying but he insisted after he insulted me. Whatever, it doesn't matter."

"What do you mean he insulted you?" he asks through clenched teeth. The guys in his team step forward to listen as Nate walks closer with pure rage in his eyes.

I look down at my Doc Martens and then look back at him. "He said that it would be a shame for you to treat me the same way you treat the girls you go out with..." I trail off.

"I'm listening. Go on," he says sarcastically.

Getting irritated by his sarcastic tone, I say it loud enough for everyone to hear, tired of this charade.

"He said it hasn't been long since your last fight, when you were making out with that girl, whose breasts you autographed in the back." His head snaps up, looking guilty, and I know Maverick was telling the truth.

"It's okay. Really. We're not together or anything. I know it's not like that, I'm no different." He frowns at the hurt look on my face. "You can stop feeling sorry for me now," I snap.

"Giselle, don't. That's not true," Brie says behind me. She says it knowing I'm done fighting, done holding on. I don't care what anyone thinks of me. I want to be alone.

I walk away, going outside to the car. I get inside, pressing the button of the ignition and starting the car. My eyes are full of unshed tears that I can't let fall.

I let the tears fall down my cheeks as I drive toward the mountains on the dirt roads. I pull over, and climb until I reach a height that offers the view of the skyline. I try to gain my footing and stand on a ledge so I can see the depths of darkness below. Getting as close as I can with my boots, I look down and wonder. All it would take is a slight push, a slight jump, and it'll over. The pain would be all over. I could bask in the darkness, forget, and finally sleep. I turn around and Nate is standing there with a look of genuine fear on his face.

Tendrils of my hair fly in the wind as I look at him with tears sliding down my eyes.

"I don't feel sorry for you. I need you and I can't be without you. You're mine and you will always be mine. I lied about telling everyone we were together just to protect you. I wanted the world to know you were by my side, that you are mine. I was afraid you wouldn't want that with me."

I stand there silently, listening to his words, and moving toward him, away from the ledge. His face looks relieved as he opens his arms and I melt into his embrace. He walks me down the mountain to the car, and I see he came after me on his motorcycle. He opens the door of the car and slides in the driver's side to turn it on. The cold air comes out of the air vents, then he gets out and opens the rear passenger door. He motions for me to lie in the back seat, face down, with my jean-clad ass in the air. He pulls my low jeans down my ass and slides my thong to the side. Not even checking if I'm wet, he takes his erect cock, slides it into my tight pussy, and we both moan. He stretches me inside, mixing his pain with pleasure. We fit so well together, like we were made for each other. He begins pounding into me, pulling my hair out the confines of my messy bun on the top of my head.

"I didn't fuck that girl that day or anyone after you. I have only had you since the first time. I've only wanted this pussy, it's the one I enjoy milking my cock," he says, pounding into me in a delicious rhythm. "I want you so much, Giselle. I will always want you, baby. I'm jealous if another man even looks at you."

I mewl as he continues to pull my hair. I stick my ass out higher to meet his thrusts, the wave of an orgasm building higher and higher as he pounds into me. It's so deep, I can feel him everywhere. You can hear the slap of his hips against my ass as he takes me with my face down on the seat. He slowly caresses my waist until he's grabbing the globes of my ass, fucking me raw. He gives me pleasure on the side of the road by the mountain, with the rays of sunset turning the sky to twilight, the onset of night, shrouding the day in total darkness.

We both cum at the same time, moaning, our orgasm meeting each other's in sync. It's raw and beautiful. I forget that any car that passes by this road will see us. He pulls my jeans back up and puts himself away, helping me stand on my shaking legs. I turn to face him and he softly kisses my lips.

"Even in death," he breathes.

His forehead is against mine and I know he's referencing the night he watched me dance. I thought he couldn't see me, that the depths of my lost soul were invisible to him as he watched me. I realize he can see me, even when I can't see in the darkness of my lost soul.

I drive, following him in the car behind his bike back to the house. We take a shower together and wash each other. When I reach his thighs, he looks down and takes my hand, placing my fingers over his scars.

"My father used to wake me up every day to get ready for school by burning my thighs with cigarettes after my mother died. Every day, I would wake up to the feeling and the smell of cigarettes. The burns would swell and sting with pain the whole day. He would do it there, so no one could see any evidence that I was being abused."

My eyes fill with tears, picturing him as a little boy suffering in pain every day. I kneel, kissing every scar on his thighs, swirling my tongue under the spray of water. He looks down at me with tenderness and he knows I'm doing the same thing he did when I had all the bruises on my body. The way he would kiss them gently, giving pleasure where there is pain. He raises me up by my hands, with the water dripping down my naked body. I can see his tortured soul within his eyes, trusting me enough to tell me where his demons came from.

On the bed, I lay my head on his chest, caressing his

stomach lightly with my fingers, taking in his scent. His arms hold me, giving me warmth. He begins to speak, telling me more.

"My mother was a heroin addict. She never hit me, and hardly fed or bathed me. I learned all on my own how to take care of myself. I would come home from school to a mother high on her poison. When my father would come home, she was so out of it, she couldn't feel the beating he would give her. My father was a meth addict, but also a drunk. He would come home almost every night and beat me after my mother died. They brought me up on pain and it's the only thing I know."

Tears slide down my cheeks at how brutal his life was, understanding the need to sleep alone. The trauma and pain he experienced all his life is gut wrenching. I wouldn't have survived it. I'm amazed he survived the pain, the scars, and the torture his own parents inflicted on him since the day he was born. To know that the people who should love you more than life itself, could cause you to live and breathe in so much pain. To only know pain and not love is the biggest curse of all, living inside yourself in total darkness. The only thing that matters is the darkness and the demons trying to take you every night when you close your eyes, meeting the hounds of Hell. I weep as the tears fall like blood, sliding down his chest for his trapped soul in pain.

"What happened to your mom?" I sniff, wiping my face in a shaky breath.

"She died overdosing while my father was beating her, disfiguring her face on the floor when I came home from school one afternoon. He threatened me, told me to call the cops and say we found her like that. I did what he asked. I covered for him when the cops came, out of fear that I would end up just like her. He threatened me with a promise and I knew it was all my fault. I helped him cover up my mother's death. He continued to beat and abuse me. One day, before I turned thirteen, drug dealers killed him. They came to collect, knowing he wouldn't pay them. I was sent to foster care, and learned to fight the kids who bullied me, because I had nothing and was broke. They made fun of my clothes, shoes, and told me I was nothing. They even said that my parents didn't want me. I met Jaden at the Y. The guys on my team were all from foster care just like I was, it's where they taught kids like us self-defense. I'm obviously good at it, and it helped me cope with my pain. The pain I feel every day of my life, I take it there, in the cage. I started street fighting in underground warehouses. Jaden uploaded my fights on social media and got the attention of MMA promoters. They gave me a shot, and it paid off. My life revolves around pain and it's all I know. It's who I am, giving me release from the nightmares that come, a way to dull my pain, and it's all that mattered, until you."

I look up from lying on his muscular chest into his eyes and I understand what he means. He hasn't had nightmares since I've been here, sleeping with him every night.

"Did you have one last night?

"Yes, every time you're not here, they come."

"I'm so sorry, Nate. I promise not to leave you."

"You can never leave me. I'm with you, inside you."

I kiss him softly as he wipes my tears.

"Will you walk with me to the cage at the fight by my side?" he asks.

"If you want me to, I'll be there. Always."

We fall asleep. Tonight, the nightmares don't come, being in the Reaper's arms, having him hold me, because without him, I am a lost soul, dying alone, wishing for his love.

18
GISELLE

We arrive at the hotel where the fight event is being held in Vegas. The crowd is loud, with wild, screaming fans holding signs cheering for their fighter. Pictures of the Grim Reaper and a ballerina are everywhere. The fans sell out every seat for the expecting match between Maverick De Leon and Nate "The Reaper" Phoenix. I scan the excited crowd and see flashing lights from their camera phones looking at the commentators, with the judges reporting the fighters' stats on who is expected to win. I can even see the drawings from Nate's fans with my name written in glitter. I stand back, waiting for the door to open and Brie to come through. Jaden and Nate are inside with the doctors, clearing him before the fight. The door opens and the doctor nods on his way out for us to enter. Nate is standing ready, with a dark, hooded cloak like the Grim Reaper. A direct contrast to my white tank top with my name glittered in pink, feminine and delicate. I'm wearing my low-cut skinny jeans and my boots, ready to walk by the Reaper's side toward the cage to deal with his pain, and feed his demons. Jaden and Brie will walk behind with the rest of his team as one unit. We are all anxiously waiting for security to walk us through for his introduction to the fight. I am nervous about him fighting. What if he gets seriously hurt? I know this is who he is, but if something happens to him in there with Maverick, I wouldn't be able to bear it. Maverick wants to take his title, the look of him in the cage, walking around it like a caged animal, screaming, baring his teeth while the crowd cheers and boos.

I look over and the security gives us the signal to move forward and enter. *Invincible* by Pop Smoke plays in the background as Nate's intro song as we walk toward the cage. The crowd goes wild, screaming his name, and trying to grab us. Security stops rowdy fans from trying to put their hands on us, shoving them back further and my steps falter. Nate slows down and grabs my hand as he removes his hooded cloak, giving it to Jaden. He looks down, his face inches closer, and kisses me on my lips. His hands are in my hair, the fans scream in the background, cheering him on. He breaks the kiss, leaving me to walk with Brie to the front seats reserved with security.

He gets inside the cage with his shorts bearing the signature Grim Reaper logo with all his hard muscles on display. The referee brings them together to read them the rules. Suddenly, Maverick turns to where I'm sitting, blows me a kiss, and gives me a wink. Nate lunges forward, baring his teeth containing his mouthpiece. Jaden runs inside the cage to hold him back. I get up from my seat and Nate looks at me through the cage. The crowd and cameras look my way. I blow him a kiss with my hand, and mouth 'always.' The commentator above, showcasing the fight speaks through the mic, "Did she mouth 'always?' Well, whatever she said seemed to calm Nate 'The Reaper' as he is back to his corner, ready to begin the fight."

I sit back down in my seat, holding Brie's hand, hoping for the best with my nerves on edge. The bell dings and Nate springs forward, forcefully kicking Maverick in the stomach. Maverick flies back with force against the cage, stunned. Nate goes after him, and reins blow after blow on Maverick's face with pent up rage. Maverick's, whose face is swelling up like a balloon, catches his balance, grabs Nate by the waist, and straddles him to the ground. My stomach drops, my heart beating like a million galloping horses, and my adrenaline makes me shake on the edge of my seat. Nate blocks the blows but some land on his beautiful face, splitting his lip, and brow. He smiles manically while the blood oozes down his face and his chest. Maverick looks confused and drops his arm for a split second. Nate sees the opportunity to elbow him on the side of his face. Maverick falls back and Nate gets up, looking like he was a victim of a massacre. He wipes the blood off as the bell rings, ending the first round. In his corner, Jaden is there, talking to him and stopping the bleeding. He tells him something I can't hear as the seconds count down to the start of the second round. My heart beat slows down to a mild tempo as Nate seems to be okay. When the bell rings and he gets up, my heart speeds up all over again. Brie holds my hand as I stare, transfixed, at Nate's movement in the cage. He switches between boxing, judo, using a combination of jujitsu, and Muay Thai. He goes for his legs, Maverick falters, his knee giving out, and the crowd goes wild. Nate moves in with a series of blows, knocking Maverick out cold for the KO. Relieved, I stand up, cheering and excitedly hug Brie. I turn my head, looking in the direction if the cage and see the doctors rush to check on Maverick, while Nate hugs his team and remains undefeated. He turns to me after the official acknowledges the win broadcasted live, jumping over the cage, straddling it, and calling us over. Security escorts us up and he jumps down. I rush into his arms, not caring that he's full of blood and sweat. I look down, watching his blood stain my shirt in big, red, angry blotches, bleeding into my skin. He gives me a black hoodie with his logo on it and I put it on. I look at him, seeing his happiness at his win, but my eyes reflect the hurt I feel for the wounds on his face.

"I'm okay, baby. It's okay. It looks worse than it feels."

"Okay." I smile, finding him beautiful even with his face swollen.

The doctor comes to look at Nate and checks him out. The doctor nods that he is okay and sends him to get stitches.

We get home and I help him shower as he sits on the teak bench. I remove my clothes, dropping them to the floor, and quickly get to work on washing the sweat and blood from his body. I can see the beginnings of bruises showing their black and blue hues through his skin. I carefully wash his face as he sits quietly, watching me care for him, the water from the shower masking the tears filling my eyes. I blink my tears away as they begin to fall for his pain.

"Don't cry for me."

"I will always cry when you're hurt for fear that you will be gone one day."

He tries for a smile but winces as the cut on his lips splits open, making blood ooze down his chin.

He spits on the shower floor, letting the blood flow like a river on the slate black tiles. I help him clean the wound and finish washing myself as he stands slowly. His hands touch my breasts and my nipples stand erect, aroused. He continues lower, passing my belly to the apex of my thighs, dipping a finger between my folds. He slides his middle finger in my hot, wet pussy, ready for him, getting enough of my juice so he can taste it with his tongue.

"Hmm. Always so good," he says, closing his eyes and savoring the taste. I grab his hand, entwining my fingers in his, and lead him toward the bed.

19

NATE

I wake up to the same nagging pain I feel every morning after a fight. Giselle is there with a glass of water, pain meds in hand. She must have felt me stir and figured my body would feel like shit.

"Good morning. Does it… Does it hurt like this every time?"

"Yeah, depends on…if I want to take the pain or not. What I mean is, if I let them hit me. I need the pain to feel alive. I feed off it, so I won't feel bad about basically ending their career. Hence, why I got named 'The Reaper.'"

"So, this is the price you pay." She looks at my cuts and bruises softly.

"I'm used to this. I've told you. It's all I know."

"I can understand. Ballet and dance are all I know. It's all I've ever done."

She pauses as I sit up in the bed, swinging my legs out, the pain not as bad.

"Do you need help to get to the bathroom?"

"I'm good, doesn't really hurt. Thank you for bringing me water and my meds."

She sees me moving the sheets so I can stand, then she

kneels in front of me on the side of the bed so she can move my slides. She looks up slowly, on her knees, into my eyes and I can't help myself. I'm in love with her. If she only knew how much I love her. I didn't know if I could ever feel love and it's only for her that I feel this way. I can't be without her. I need her. I desperately hope she feels the same, at least enough for her to stay. She stands and I bring her close so I can lie my head on her flat stomach to breathe her in, and the sweet feminine smell of her perfume. I look up and she smiles down at me.

"I love you," I tell her softly. She stays silent, staring at me with her beautiful mouth slightly open, and steps back as I get up. I walk to the bathroom, feeling her stare on my back as I close the door. I look at my reflection in the bathroom mirror. I close my eyes, not used to the feeling of loving someone with the fear of losing them. When she was on the ledge about to jump off, I felt fear. The gut-wrenching fear of darkness that I couldn't come back from if I lost her because if I felt fear, I knew that I loved her.

When she turned and came back to me, I looked into her eyes, seeing the demons inside looking for darkness. Darkness I could provide so that she could dance in the light.

20
GISELLE

I stare at the closed door, stunned at his last words. Words I've longed to hear from his lips. I know I should have told him how I felt. If he only knew I love him, I dance for him, and I always want to be with him, always. It's too late though. I know if I walk in there, he will retreat inside himself. I will give him time to process his feelings and show my love for him, because even through my lost soul in the darkness, he's there, waiting.

I open the closet door inside the dressing room for the first time. Once inside, I glance at all the rows of his designer clothes. I walk further and to the right I see all the dance outfits he's laid out for me every morning since I came back. The Chanel dress, lingerie, shoes, every item carefully placed. I run my fingers through the fine silk, tracing the delicate patterns of dresses I could never afford. On the center island lies a white letter-sized envelope with my name. I curiously look over, grab the envelope, and open it. I scan the document that reveals the dance studio purchased in my name from Lenora.

My eyes fill with unshed tears of happiness that I finally have the dream of my dance studio. Nate has given me everything I have ever wanted, especially his love. I knew I would trade it all just to have his love. I quickly place the papers back into the envelope, place it exactly as it was, and quickly dress in designer black joggers with a white crop top.

I'm in the kitchen making scrambled eggs and pancakes I found in the fully stocked kitchen, when Nate appears. He smiles with a raised eyebrow. "I didn't know you could cook?"

"There are a lot of things you don't about me," I say, playfully.

"I know all the important stuff," he says. I giggle.

"I grew up on a farm and if you wanted to eat, you needed learn how to cook. My mom and dad taught me a lot, since I was homeschooled. My mom cooked every day, but one day I watched and really learned."

"They must have been amazing."

"Yeah, they were," I say sadly.

"I want to take you out today."

I place the plate of food in front of him and he looks at the perfect eggs and fluffy pancakes. I sit next to him on the island. "Okay. But I'm driving since you're taking pain meds."

"Fine. By the way, this is delicious."

I smile, loving the fact that he likes my cooking. He finishes, leaving nothing on the plate. I wash the dishes, placing everything back in place, ready with keys in hand. He walks behind me, sliding his hand on my ass and pulls me close so I can feel his erection in front of the Bentley.

"Every time I look at this car it reminds me of taking you in the back seat," he whispers in my ear. I close my eyes, remembering how we both came undone on the side of the road.

"Now we have to do the same to all your cars. Especially the bike."

"That can be arranged," he says, getting into the passenger side of the car.

He inputs an address into the GPS, and I turn the car out in the direction it gives me. We arrive at the address of a ballet theatre in Vegas.

"Why are we here?

"I need you to talk to someone who is expecting you."

He opens the car door after I park, with his hoodie over his head, hiding his stitches on the swollen part of his face.

I follow him to the administration office of the building to a door that reads 'Director.' He knocks, placing his hand in mine, lacing our fingers. I look at him curiously as the door swings open and a middle-aged lady stands smiling.

"You must be Giselle. My name is Anna, the Director of pre-professional ballet and contemporary dance."

I stay speechless as she turns to Nate. "Hello, Mr. Phoenix. Welcome, if you can please have a seat." She motions to the seats in front of her desk as she steps back inside her office, allowing us to take a seat.

"It is a pleasure to have you come by and bring Giselle. I am excited to discuss the possibility for Giselle to assist us with pre-professional dance instruction."

She turns to look at me.

"Giselle, I have heard about your exceptional talent. I think with your skills, you would be an asset to our program. I would like to offer you the opportunity to be part of our program and the ability to use our theatre for events with your students. In addition, an opportunity for you to be part of the performances. You have exceptional skill and talent."

I am stunned. This is what I have always wanted. I look at Nate and he grins at the look on my face.

"If you need time to think about..."

"I accept," I say, cutting her off.

She smiles. "Perfect. I'm excited to have you join and be part of our program. You'll be compensated for your instruction and performances. I will send all the details to your manager, Giselle."

"I don—"

Nate gets up quickly, cutting me off to shake Anna's hand. "Yes, send all the details to her manger. Thank you."

I get up from the chair and shake her hand, not understanding. Who is my manager? I know this is all Nate's doing. I know he is surprising me and it's all I've ever wanted, but I hate not having any control. We walk, after we say our goodbyes, toward the car. "What was that all about?"

"The best opportunity instead of going back to New York."

"What are you talking about?"

"Since the video and the hype with fight, you and me together, they have reached out to Jaden about you. They have offered you opportunities to join or work in contemporary dance to ballet. Many production companies, theaters, you name it, even The Porcelain Dollhouse wants you to have a final dance night. Kind of like a sendoff, Jaden is getting bombarded. Your manager is Brie and I don't think you would object. She will handle everything since she is with Jaden all the time. She can help you with the dance studio and to promote it. The manager at The Porcelain Dollhouse offered to promote the dance studio if you agreed to do a last dance.

I look at him, surprised at everything they have planned and done for me. I feel like crying, not because of what is happening inside, but for being lucky to have Nate and Brie in my life, even Jaden. They have been there for me when I have been in my darkest moments.

I place my hand on his. "I can't believe you've gone through so much trouble for me. You don't have to spend money on me or give me anything."

He raises his hand to caress my cheek, sliding his thumb over my lips. I kiss his thumb, sliding my tongue lightly.

"I'll do anything for you. I want you to smile. I miss your smile and your laughter." I close my eyes, loving his soft words.

"Okay. I'll smile for you, and I'll laugh for you. Always," I whisper, meaning every word, hoping to have the courage to tell him how much I love him. His phone rings, interrupting the moment. He answers, says a few words, and hangs up. He looks at me with determination on his face.

"Will you move in with me?"

My eyes go wide. I never thought he wanted me permanently in his house. That would mean that I would have to move here, and I was going to decide anyway with the opportunity offered because of Nate. I just never imagined moving here with Nate.

"Are you sure you want that?"

"Yes. I'm sure. I want you. I want to be with you. If you don't want that, then tell me, and I'll understand."

I inwardly sigh. "Of course I want to be with you," I say.

He releases a deep breath, lowering his lips to hover over mine, and kisses me softly with his minty breath. I move over a little, for fear I'll open the cut on his lip, but I kiss him intimately with a soft brush of my lips.

"Will you agree to dance one last time at the club? But it has to be for me," he says while tracing a finger down my hoodie. My breath quickens as the pulling need between my thighs intensifies, while his finger traces over my nipple and I squirm in the driver's seat.

"Yes, if you agree to let me rub my pussy on your cock."

"Fuck."

He closes his eyes, leaning his head back. "If you promise not to show too much when you dance."

"Okay, deal. I won't show too much when I dance, but when I come to you, I can sit on your lap, and rub my pussy on your delicious cock."

He adjusts himself in his pants, as his erection is clearly visible through his sweats. "We'd better get going before the theatre parking lot will get a show, and it won't be a dance or ballet." I giggle and he smiles. "There's my girl. I love your laugh." I stop giggling looking at his beautiful face even if it's swollen with cuts and bruises.

"For you, always."

I pull out of the parking lot onto the road. "Make a left and there is a place where we can eat lunch."

"Okay," I say, smiling, loving the fact that we can spend time together. I can't believe I agreed to move in with him. I've never lived with anyone else besides my parents and Brie. I really don't count school because that was different. I'm nervous about having an actual relationship, but it's Nate. I feel comfortable with Nate. He understands my pain, my nightmares, and my fears. He is always there to fight them.

In the back of my mind, I have the feeling he is about to do something dangerous sooner than rather than later. It's about what happened to Brie and me. I know deep down Nate and Jaden will not let them get away with it. I should think of something else and avoid them getting arrested or, worse, dead by a gunshot. Jack and his sick, drug addicted friends are cowards. They will pull a gun on them if Nate confronts them. I get nervous and my hands shake when thinking of Jack and losing Nate or Jaden. My best friend has found someone to have a relationship with, even if they aren't official. I couldn't bear it if something happened to them for something that wasn't their fault. It happened, I'm broken because of it with lasting nightmares, but it's not worth it if I lose Nate.

"What's wrong?" He frowns. "Why are you shaking?"

"What?" Lost in my thoughts, not realizing my hands were noticeably shaking on the steering wheel.

"What's wrong, baby? Your hands are shaking. What are you thinking about?"

"Nothing. It's just..." I pull into the parking lot of the café he wanted to have lunch at.

"Tell me."

"I don't want you to go after Jack and his people. I'm afraid if something bad happens to you or Jaden. Brie and I, we can't lose you both."

His eyes soften, and he kisses the palm of my hand with the tenderest of kisses. I have fallen so deeply in love with him. I get butterflies in my stomach every time I feel his touch on my skin.

"Don't worry about that. I don't want you or Brie to worry about those motherfuckers. It's taken care of. You just worry about your last dance at the club and wrapping things up at your apartment. I will have everything you want to bring sent over to the house. You have a dance studio to run. I know you saw the papers in the closet."

My eyes go wide that he knows I was going through the papers in the closet. He quickly sees my reaction.

"Relax, Giselle. I wanted you to see them. I left them there for you to find." He grins.

"I'm sorry for not thanking you. I just… I'm not used to all this, and the gifts. It's a lot." I look up, looking out the window at the busy Vegas café. I look back at him. He's silent, watching me. "Thank you for everything. I will work hard, and I appreciate everything you have done for me. I want to repay you…"

"Shh. Shh," he interrupts me. He shakes his head *no*.

"Don't. You don't have to repay me for anything. I wanted to. All I want is for you to be by my side. I know it's hard for you right now. It's enough that you're deciding to move in with me in and be by my side."

I nod my head *yes*. "Okay." I smile.

"Alright, give me a kiss and let's go eat." I kiss him softly, knowing he changed the subject about Jack. I put it in the back of my mind for now and get out to have lunch with him at the café. When we are inside to order, curious looks come our way and people taking pictures of us. "Is it always going to be like this?"

He smiles. "You have made me even more popular."

"Me?"

"Oh yeah, Money Monroe," he says playfully.

I snort in laughter at my stage name at The Porcelain Dollhouse.

"I'm the lucky one to have your attention," he says.

"I think you have more than just my attention." I smirk.

"Really? What else do I have that's more than just your attention." He slouches in the chair extending his long legs, looking sexy in his hoodie. He takes it off, revealing his tatted arm, his tight, white T-shirt against his muscled chest, filling it out completely. He catches me ogling him down to his slim waist, raising an unstitched brow.

I smile, embarrassed at getting caught checking him out. "The important parts," I say.

"Hmm. If you only knew there are only two parts that I'm interested in, but we can have that conversation another time when we're alone."

"Okay," I say, wondering what parts he's referring to.

We arrive at the house, and I decide I want to get in the pool and wear the bikini he bought for me. It's a vintage Chanel-style bikini that is more like micro bikini on purpose, by design. I walk out while he lounges by the pool, near the open french doors that lead from the pool to the bedroom. He raises his head and leans on his elbows from the lounge chair wearing designer aviator sunglasses and new, long-length shorts. I can't see his expression, but he grins in approval.

"Come here," he says. I walk over and his fingers slide between the folds of my shaved pussy through the tiny bikini bottom. My clit is throbbing from his light touch and my pussy leaks with desire. I look at what his fingers are doing hooking inside the bikini bottom, seeking the softness of my folds to the sleek wetness inside.

"You have a beautiful body and a pretty pussy," he says, huskily. My nipples strain in the small triangle top, pulling me closer, sliding his hand to caress my breasts, and my head falls to the side as I moan. He slides his legs over and gets up, towering over me as I look up into his eyes with desire. He walks me back and guides me to the sun shelf of the pool with the in-pool loungers.

He lies on one of them, leaving me standing next to him in the warm pool, the water level at my shins. He slides his shorts down, revealing his hard cock with a drop of pre-cum glistening in the sunlight. I straddle him and I slide the scrap of fabric from the bikini bottom to the side and impale myself on his cock, filling me, stretching me inch by delicious inch. We both moan as my hands lay on his hard, chiseled chest. His hands find my waist, and I ride his cock as the sun sets. My head falls back as his hands slide up, holding me by the waist as he moans. His hands find my breasts as I find a steady rhythm, dragging out the delicious sensation of my wet pussy milking his cock. His head falls back farther as he raises his hips, thrusting into me. His hands find the globe of my ass cheeks and squeezes them, opening me wider so he can sink his cock deeper inside me. I arch my back, placing my hands on his thighs as I ride us both to climax. I scream his name, moaning over and over.

"Yes, baby. You're so beautiful, cumming for me. I love to see you cum on my dick when your pussy is filled with my cock." He slides his hands on my thighs, back up to the crack of my ass until his fingers are inside my hole, using our dripping cum to coat them. He slides one finger inside and I moan.

"I feel so full," I say. He slides a second finger and I think I might die of the pleasure he is giving me. "More! Hmm. I want more," I hiss.

He licks his lips, sliding his fingers out quickly, and gets up from the lounge chair with me in his arms, walking us into the bedroom. He lays me on the bed, face down in the same position as when we were in the back seat of the Bentley. He slides the tiny bikini bottom barely covering my ass to the side, and coats his fingers with our cum to lubricate the entrance of my ass. He places the tip of his cock at the entrance of my puckered hole as two fingers slide inside my wet, pulsing pussy. I sneak a peek at him, looking back, and I can see that his sunglasses are off, eyes smoldering with desire. He pushes inside my ass and I close my eyes, reveling in the pain while his fingers pumps inside my pussy roughly as he inches his big, fat cock inside me, filling me completely.

"Nate, you feel so fucking good. Hmm," I moan. I turn and lie my head down so I can raise my ass as he pounds me. He doesn't withdraw his fingers, but keeps them inside my pussy, adding a third finger, making me feel so full. All I feel is pleasure, and the high wave of an orgasm. Nate is grunting as the slaps of our bodies come together, his cock swells inside my ass, pulsing, and my pussy floods as I cum hard, screaming his name on my lips.

"You belong to me, all of you. Giselle, you're all mine," he says, grunting until he cums with one last thrust, spilling hot cum inside my ass while his hands are holding my hips, arms bulging. He keeps thrusting in and out, riding his orgasm until every drop is inside me. He turns his head to look at his cock inside my ass.

"It's so beautiful to see my dick inside you," he whispers.

After a shower, I fall asleep on his chest with my hair sprawled in disarray. The demons don't come out to play tonight. Tonight, we turned them into art.

21
NATE

I wake up to her even breathing on my chest, and it's the most beautiful way to wake up in the morning. The girl I love in my bed with her sweet scent, keeping my demons from surfacing, knowing that the darkness is inside, and not at the surface where my angel sighs.

Jaden sets her up dancing at The Porcelain Dollhouse. I didn't lie to her about them reaching out and wanting her to come back. They did, and I told them my girl wasn't coming back to dance. She only dances like that for me. Jaden insisted I let her dance one last time, her last final at The Porcelain Dollhouse. It's the cover we need to have a motive for being there.

I will kill them in revenge for the pain they have caused, and reap their souls for the girl they have broken. Tonight, she dances in the light while I play with her demons. She stirs on my chest, and I hate to wake her, but I have to tell her to get ready. We will fly to Sioux Falls, where she and Brie can go to the apartment and pick out what they want to have sent over.

They will be driven to the club while we meet them a short while later. I'm nervous—not nervous about killing those cowards, but I am nervous about asking her, in front of the thousands of people coming to see her, to be my wife. I had a custom engagement ring made for her, it's a ballerina in a pirouette, holding a five-carat round diamond solitaire. I wanted her ring to be meaningful and beautiful, just like her. My love for her holds no bounds; it's dark and possessive, accepting her as she is, demons and all. Jaden and Brie know my intention to ask her, and they're sure she will accept. The black box holding the ring waiting to be placed on her finger is in my closet drawer. I look at her beautiful green eyes as they flutter open.

"Good morning, beautiful." She smiles.

"We leave in two hours to Sioux Falls. Are you ready for tonight?"

"Yes." She nods, her eyes holding the promise of pleasure and desire.

"Let's go."

We arrive at the private airport with Jaden, Brie, and Nick. Nick will be our third. I trust him for this sort of thing. We have had each other's back in every way possible since we were kids in high school. We leave Brie and Giselle in the blacked-out Bentley, taking them to the apartment where the movers are already waiting for them to take what they want back to Vegas. Just as planned, we will meet them in time at the club. Once the Bentley takes off with them inside, I can breathe. I don't want them to be involved in what we are about to do. The three of us dressed in all black, unmarked hoodies, black jeans, and black sneakers. "Everything in place?" I ask Jaden.

"Yeah, we have to pick up the three bikes at an unmarked location. Those fucks are in Brie's mom's trailer, operating it like a crack house. Her mother is busy working a shift. We will wait until dark, and make our move. She won't be back for three hours after it gets dark."

"Good."

"Nick, you ready?"

"Yeah brother, you know I have your back. You too, Jaden. I got you."

I confided in Nick, telling him what happened to Brie and Giselle. His eyes went wide in disbelief, wanting to kill those fuckers himself. He understood the rage, the sinister anger inside me as I told him every detail on Brie's abuse, and how they were attacked. I even told him about Giselle's nightmares every night in my arms, screaming in pain as she relives the moment. They broke her as they beat her friend and made her watch. Brie's mother was so high on drugs, she didn't even stir to see Giselle brutally raped while her daughter watched in agony with muffled screams. Biding your time is the most difficult when you want revenge. Jaden and Nick understood it.

No one touches what's mine and breathes. Maverick, I knocked the fuck out, and sent him a check for his chivalry with my girl at the store. I'll never let another man pay for what my girl wants. He knows not to fucking mention her name. Jaden paid him a brief visit after the fight, making sure he knew I fight in the cage, but am capable of killing outside like a thief in the night. Tonight is the night I will unleash and inflict the pain. Tonight, the Reaper comes to reap the souls unannounced, bringing death to those who wronged him.

The black escalade is waiting, and we head out to pick up the blacked-out motorcycles, with no markings and no tags. We head out like the hounds of Hell in the night, looking for prey. We arrive at the small trailer park off a road in the middle of nowhere. It's dark except for two lights, one leading in and one leading out to the main road. It's a fucking dump. Only crack heads and drug dealers live in these types of trailers. It reminds me of where I grew up, the stench of old garbage, and stale cigarettes everywhere. We park our motorcycles out of sight, far enough from the trailer that belongs to Brie's mom.

A pickup truck and Camaro is parked out of place in front of the trailer. I'm eager to rip them to shreds knowing they're inside, where they brutally raped her. I see the same look on Jaden's face. He's imagining that piece of shit doing the same to Brie. Nick looks at us both, feeling the radiating energy of hate and vengeance we're giving off.

We take out masks and don them over our heads, replacing the hood of our hoodies. The tight fabric with skulls, marking our faces like death in the night. We each have our Glocks and intricate knives in holsters around our stomachs. Jaden throws us each a rope and a chain. We nod and walk quietly toward the trailer.

We can see light and movement through the dirty, broken blinds. There's three of them inside. We will each take one, but Jack is mine. The burley one with a protruding stomach and greasy hair. It's the same guys we saw at the club. There is only one entrance into the trailer.

Nick and Jaden stay hidden on the side while I knock on the door. Once I knock, I hear movement.

"Who is it?" Jack asks through the door. I stay silent, and knock again until he opens the door and we can ambush him. I have my hand on the Glock in the back of my pants, ready to pull it out and place it on his head once I kick the door when he unlocks it.

"Who is it?" he repeats angrily, unlocking the door, not knowing torture and death are waiting for him.

Once I hear the click of the door unlocking, it's our signal to ambush the trailer. I kick the door with full force, Jack staggers back in surprise, the door hitting him in the face as he howls in pain. He reaches for his face as the crack of bone from the door has blood sliding down his face. The other two are stunned and caught off guard while Jaden and Nick rush inside. They tie them up with rope on their knees, execution style, while they watch me place the Glock on Jack's forehead.

"Ready to meet your maker, motherfucker?" I say.

"Who are you? What do you want?" he says shakily.

I turn my head. Nick and Jaden have the other two gagged and kneeling with a gun to their head.

I look back at Jack's greasy disgusting face. "I told you I'll come for you. You took something from me," I say through clenched teeth.

"If it's money or drugs, I have nothing to do with it. I can give you what you want... Just leave us alone and get the fuck out."

Fucking coward. "Nah. It's not about drugs or money. I don't need drugs, and I have plenty of money. You took something that didn't belong to you. You also took something from him that was never yours to take." I point at Jaden. His eyes go wide, realizing I'm talking about Giselle and Brie.

"They're just some whores that dance in a club. What do you rich guys care about, some small-town pussy?"

I push the barrel of the gun as the rage inside me boils to the surface at him, calling them whores. "Call them whores one more time, motherfucker. You fucking raped them, you piece of shit. Now you will pay." I take out the wicked knife from the holster. His eyes go wide as the other two muffle in screams.

"What the fuck are you going to do with that?"

"Something that I've had to wait too long to do." I slice his face in pieces, watching the flesh split open, oozing blood, spilling crimson in the trailer's stench. All the old memories come flooding back of my childhood rage. He tries to scream as I hold his mouth with my gloved hand, silencing him. He falls to his knees trying to hold his face, revealing the bone underneath. I roll him on his back, and begin to slice his body, gutting him like a fish. I make sure to hit no major organs as I want him to suffer. His eyes roll back in pain, his greasy skin from his face dangling, and his disgusting teeth on display.

"You like to rape our girls. I'll show you what it feels like to be raped." His mouth gurgles with blood, spluttering. I pull off his disgusting pants with the stench of his body odor making me want to puke. I grab his pathetic excuse of a cock, take out another knife, and slice it open down to his balls as he bleeds out, twitching in the shock of pain. I look over at Jaden and Nick, watching me, as the two other guys are screaming, muffled in terror.

"Get to it! Don't forget to cut it off."

They both nod, taking revenge in doing the same. I turn back to Jack, and he is within an inch of his pathetic life. I get to work for another hour, mutilating his body in pieces. I stomp on his face, disfiguring it, shoving his pathetic cock in his mouth. Once we are done, we clean up, and make sure we leave nothing that can trace it back to us.

Jaden and Nick walk out, proud of their handiwork. We step out in the dark and ride into the night to a spot, burning our clothes to ashes. I change into a black T-shirt that says 'The Reaper,' black jeans, and designer sneakers.

We leave the motorcycles with Jaden's people, then we take off and ride back in the Escalade to the club. We are let in the side door to the back showers. The owner is friends with Jaden and our solid alibi for tonight. Brie and Giselle are with Jake, according to security. We shower and dress quickly, walking out to our awaiting table in the front VIP section. I sit down with the black box containing the engagement ring in my front pocket.

I spot Brie and Giselle talking to Jake, most likely about her choice of song. The club is full of athletes and fans. I even see Jace and Jason at a table to the right. They nod and salute us with their drinks in hand. I stare with a glare, rolling my eyes. "Yeah, in your dreams," I mutter under my breath. People go live on social media showing the stage where Giselle will perform her final dance at The Porcelain Dollhouse. Some fans are even taking pictures of us from afar. I bet they're having a field day posting about tonight. Jaden said that there are no more spaces to sign up for Giselle's dance studio. I smile at her from my table and she smiles, waving and blowing me a kiss. I mouth, 'always.' Even from here, I can tell she's blushing.

The club is playing *Enjoy Yourself* by Pop Smoke in the background, waiting for Jake to announce Giselle. The strippers are on the side, dancing for other customers.

I look at Nick and Jaden ordering drinks, then Nick looks at me.

"She's the one, isn't she?"

I nod my head. "Yeah, she is. I just hope she feels the same."

"Brother, that was fucking crazy," he says excitedly. I know he is referring to what we did and how I took care of our minor problem. Jaden is looking at Brie, talking to Jake animatedly with her hands, his hands balled up into fists with jealousy.

"Relax," I tell him, "you know she wants you."

"Right now, it doesn't look like it." He points up toward them by the DJ booth. I chuckle.

"Who would have thought you would fall for someone? You're worse than I am in that regard. You don't even take them to your house, except her." I grin.

"Look who's talking," he scoffs.

We both chuckle and Nick joins in.

"Are you ready to lay your ass out there for her?" Jaden asks.

"Yep, I'm ready." I'm ready to accept her even if she says no. I love her that much. The lights dim and it's time.

The spotlight is on the stage and I'm nervous as fuck. Phones are out, recording, there's people cheering, the smell of marijuana, perfume, and alcohol is in the air. Jake is on the mic, introducing Giselle.

"It's time for her final night at The Porcelain Dollhouse, her last dance inside the building. The beautiful, the talented Giselle, but here you know her as Miss Money Monroe! Make it rain, beautiful." Money falls like rain from the air from the celebrity athletes and fans she has gained.

They chant her name. I smile because deep down I know she

dances for me. Whatever song she's dancing to, is always for me. *Cherry* by Lana del Rey plays through the sound system. She is on the top of the pole. She slides upside down, dressed all in white lingerie with garters and suede, platform boots. My heart stops at how beautiful she looks with her hair down and her red, cherry lips.

My cock is fucking hard in my pants. She comes to me and sits on my lap, true to her word, rubbing her pussy on my cock, and her hands on my chest. My heart beats loudly, and she bends to show me her panties marking her pussy. I grab her ass, gliding my hands up to her waist. She turns to me as the song breaks, why she falls to pieces when she is with me. The crowd in the background record us, the lights from their phones shining in the darkness. She glides her hands up to my face, kisses me softly, and the song echoes that she loves me, the love and desire plain on her face.

"I love you," she says as the song ends. I grab the black box in my pocket, and she frowns for a split second, then her eyes widen as she realizes it's a jewelry box.

The spotlight in the club is on us as I open the box, looking at her. "Will you marry me?" I ask her softly. The entire room goes silent, waiting for her answer. I am nervous even though she told me she loves me, and it lifts a pressure in my chest.

"Even in death, I would love to be your wife." I smile, sliding the five-carat diamond custom ring on her finger, glittering in the light, getting up and holding her in my arms as she straddles her legs on my waist. The crowd cheers and roars in the background. I smile while I'm trying to cover her ass with my hands.

"Let's go home," I tell her.

She has tears in her eyes from happiness. She lowers her head and peppers kisses all over my face, trying to miss my stitches. I don't care if they open. I'll bleed out for her just to feel her love from her soft lips. She slides down, turning to hug Brie as she congratulates her.

"Okay. Let's go," she says.

We walk past the billiard section of the club where the breaking news reports our engagement from social media.

"Wow, that was fast," Brie says. The news changes to another breaking story where Brie's mother appears with a reporter in handcuffs, saying that her boyfriend and his friends, a local drug dealer by the name of Jack, have been found mutilated and castrated. Both Brie and Giselle look at us with wide eyes.

"Looks like someone took care of them for us," I say, shrugging my arms.

They stare at the news reporter, noting that Brie's mom has been arrested for drugs found in the trailer in her possession. A drug deal gone wrong. There are no witnesses or suspects.

"She's better off," Brie says, feeling no remorse for her mother as she looks at the screen.

Giselle stares at my expression. I look into her eyes, and she knows. She knows the Reaper came to collect, making good on his promise. She then looks at Nick and Jaden, realizing that they were involved, too.

22

GISELLE

My heart is full of love for Nate, my protector, and my future husband. I knew he would seek revenge for what they did to me and Brie, I just never knew it would be that painful and brutal. He inflicted pain on to those who unleashed the demons inside me. They can never physically hurt us again. I may have my demons, my nightmares and memories, but Nate will always be by my side, fighting them off. He is my darkness, and I am his light. Together, we can find our way to each other, even in death.

THE END

TO MY READERS

Thank you for choosing my book and I hope you enjoyed Giselle as much as I did writing it. I love writing Romance and mixing it up. Please leave a review on Amazon, BookBub, or Goodreads. It really helps authors understand their audience and improve their writing.

Website: www.carmenrosales.com for future releases and sign up for my VIP list.

More from Author Carmen Rosales
Elysium Trilogy Box Set- E-book and Paperback

Coming soon
Brianna-Brianna & Jaden

Hillside King Series
Hidden Scars -April 14th 2022
Hidden Lies
Hidden Secret
Hidden Truths

Dirty Little Secrets
Changing the Game

ACKNOWLEDGMENTS

I want to thank Indie Sage PR for an amazing book cover that captures my characters and for all the support they have given me as an author. I am truly humbled. Thank you to all the bloggers and my Beta readers.

ABOUT THE AUTHOR

Carmen Rosales is an emerging author of Steamy Dark Romance. Writing Alphas. Like never before. Join her VIP list- www.carmenrosales.com

She loves spending time with her family. When she is not writing, she is reading. She is an Army veteran and is currently completing her Doctorate Degree in Business and has the love and support of her husband and five children. She loves to see a review and interact with her readers. Follow her on TIKTOK at https://vm.tiktok.com/ZMRKBTbxY/

facebook.com/CarmenRosalesAuthor
twitter.com/AuthorCRosales
instagram.com/carmenrosalesauthor
bookbub.com/profile/carmen-rosales
amazon.com/~/e/B09BG3NYNX

Lightning Source UK Ltd.
Milton Keynes UK
UKHW010803060223
416537UK00008B/1728